Cornflower's Ghost

Cornflower's Ghost is a vastly entertaining novel, replete with mysterious deaths, romantic intrigues, political deceits and historical schemes covering more than 200 years. Implicated in these antics are professors and graduate students at a modern university, 1960s radicals, leaders of the American Revolution, 18th century politicians, and the specter of an Iroquois ghost. Thomas Pullyblank weaves this tale with a keen eye for detail and a storyteller's gift. But there's more than just a good story here: at the center of *Cornflower's Ghost* is history itself, and how we use the past to define ourselves and give meaning to our current struggles. Amid all the intrigue and suspense, Pullyblank's characters are fighting to claim the past and to understand it, since only history can reveal the answers to the secrets at the heart of *Cornflower's Ghost*. It's a novel that pulls you in and keeps you thinking long after you've turned the last page.

—*Brian Carso, J. D., Ph. D., Assistant Professor of History, Misericordia University*

Pullyblank's intricate tale of love, betrayal, lies, and murder cleverly weaves past and present in ways that will change the way we think about history. In fast-moving episodes full of plot twists and turns he deftly explores a fascinating region of the country – upstate New York – and the characters that have had parts both major and minor in the unfolding drama of the state's history. Importantly, *Cornflower's Ghost* is a vivid reminder that the past is always with us, and it profoundly affects how we live in the present and how we shape the future.

—*Paul D'Ambrosio, Ph. D., Vice President and Chief Curator, New York State Historical Association*

Cornflower's Ghost

Cornflower's Ghost

An Historical Mystery

Thomas Pullyblank

Square Circle Press
Voorheesville, New York

Cornflower's Ghost:
An Historical Mystery

Published by
Square Circle Press LLC
137 Ketcham Road
Voorheesville, NY 12186
www.squarecirclepress.com

First paperback edition 2009.
Printed and bound in the United States of America on acid-free, durable paper.
15 14 13 12 11 10 09   1 2 3 4 5

ISBN 13: 978-0-9789066-5-8
ISBN 10: 0-9789066-5-9
Library of Congress Control Number: 2009934094

Publisher's Acknowledgments
The cover design is by Richard Vang, Square Circle Press, using the Corel suite of graphics software. The text of this book was created and formatted by Square Circle Press using OpenOffice.org, a free suite of office software (www.openoffice.org). The title is set in CasablancaAntique, the type is in Garamond, the chapter headings in Blackadder ITC, and the chapter epigraphs in Book Antiqua.

The author's personal and professional acknowledgments appear at the end of the preface.

*Dedicated to all the instructors
at the University at Albany
who taught me to love history,
but to love life more.*

Preface

CORNFLOWER'S GHOST IS A WORK OF FICTION. Its seed was a ghost story I told one night to a group of friends on the shore of Collins Lake in Scotia, New York many years ago. Like Mary Shelley, whose own ghost story told to friends on the shore of another lake developed into one of the world's most beloved novels, I was encouraged by friends to cultivate the seed into a book. And so I watered the story and fertilized it, pruned it here and there, and although the resulting fruit comes nowhere near the blue ribbon perfection of Mary Shelley's *Frankenstein*, I do hope *Cornflower's Ghost* provides you with at least a bit of tasty reading pleasure. Cultivating the story has certainly given me much enjoyment over the years.

Cornflower's Ghost is also a work of imagined history. The American Revolution and the long shadow it cast over the nineteenth century, the "Second American Revolution" of the 1960's and its consequences still being revealed, the complex history of a family, the institutional history of a university's academic department: these histories are the soil and air, the rain and sun (and, of course, the manure) that caused the ghost story to grow from a seed into a fruit bearing plant. The history *is* history. You can go to a library or go online and find all kinds of information about these and all the other historical topics dealt with in the book.

But what you will not find is information on Theodorick Crane or any of his descendants, Mary Strong or any of hers, Albert Hartman or Benjamin Fries, Roger Whittaker,

Peter Langley or anyone in the Radisson family. The people in the story are my invention and mine alone, and I take full responsibility for their actions and indiscretions.

While I can take ownership of the material between the covers of this book, I could not have written it without the help and guidance of many friends, colleagues and family members. Thank you to Sharon Corna who typed early versions of the story back when my computer skills were non-existent; to my family in Caledonia, who support me always in everything I do; to Professors Warren Roberts, Kendall Birr and Kevin Shanley at the University at Albany, without whom I'd probably still be selling replacement vinyl windows; to Mary Linnane, John Kincheloe, Andy Coates and other graduate school friends who listened to my stories and read parts or all of this one; to Richard Vang of Square Circle Press, editor, publisher, Brother and friend; and to Kristin and Bradon Pullyblank, who throughout the later stages of this project helped me live the life my instructors taught me to love.

Cornflower's Ghost

Chapter One

*A cold coming they had of it, at this time of the
year . . . The ways deep, the weather sharp, the days
short, the sun farthest off in* solstitio brumali, *the
very dead of Winter.*

—Lancelot Andrews, *Of the Nativity*, 1622

ON MOST WINTER DAYS I STILL REMEMBER that coldest of winter
mornings, and the memory always brings with it equally
numbing recollections of Peter Langley's death and my first
encounter with Julianne Radisson. It was a record low that
morning, my first day back after a semester's leave of absence, and I was standing outside the door of Hammond
Hall, just before eight o'clock, waiting for someone inside to
unlock the door. The sky was clear and blue, almost purple
along the western horizon. The warmth I'd generated on my
walk to campus was gone. I could feel the cold air work its
way through my anorak, scarf, and mittens and prick against
my skin. As the carillon at the center of campus chimed out
the alma mater I kicked myself for returning my key before
I took time off.

I peered through the window and knocked hard on the
door. Through the fog of condensation I saw my reflection
—my brown hair looking black and my blue eyes looking
gray—and finally saw Roger Whittaker, the history department chair whose phone call had gotten me out of bed, approach from the direction of his office. He wore his usual

outfit, a gray three piece suit just a shade lighter than his close-cropped hair. When he got to the door he flung it open with a force that startled me. I jumped back to avoid being hit in the chest.

Whittaker looked me over and cocked his head. The muscles that ran up his neck and behind his ears reminded me of the straps on an old leather football helmet.

"Did you walk?" he asked.

"Dead battery," I said as I stepped inside and closed the door.

"I see," he said. He ran his hand over his hair. "I have bad news, Flanagan."

"What?" I asked.

"In my office."

I followed him around the corner and sat down across from him at the anteroom table. He pushed a newspaper my way. I removed my mittens, used my scarf to wipe my glasses, and was blindsided by the following article on page one of the *Clinton Falls Clarion*:

University Professor Dead After Late Night Automobile Crash
Alcohol Use Involved

Peter Langley, a Professor of History at the State University, is dead after suffering traumatic injuries to the head and body in an alcohol related automobile accident.

Police say Dr. Langley was traveling westbound on State Route 5 sometime between 10 and 11 p.m. when his car hit a patch of ice and slid off the road and onto the frozen Westcott Creek. Unconscious and with severe injuries to the head and back, Dr. Langley was taken to Wildwood Medical Center, where he expired at 12:13 a.m. this morning.

Dr. Frank Weston of Wildwood told the *Clarion* that Professor Langley's blood alcohol content was well above legal limits. The Clinton Falls police department confirmed that an empty bottle of vodka was found at the scene of the accident, but would not elaborate on this information and said an investigation was pending.

Since arriving at the university in 1976, Dr. Langley has been widely recognized as one of the most engaging and entertaining lecturers on campus. He is most famous for his course "Forms of Political Protest" in which he led students in hands-on demonstrations against the university administration. The course was canceled after the Randy Bucci shooting incident in December.

"He was good-natured about FPP," said the university president. "He always kept his protests civilized, the Bucci incident notwithstanding. At the same time he showed students how they, as individuals, could make a difference.

"The accident is tragic. I speak for the entire campus community when I say that Dr. Langley's presence will be missed."

Professor Langley's contribution to higher education was recognized in 1994 when he was awarded the Distinguished Teaching Professorship, an honor granted to only three other professors in the university's thirty years of existence.

No funeral or memorial services are planned. Donations can be sent to the Clinton Falls Ambulance Emergency Fund.

"He called me yesterday," I said. "He said he couldn't wait to get back at it."

"I'm sorry, Tom," Whittaker said.

Then I looked again at the headline. "This can't be right," I said.

"What?"

"Langley didn't drink."

Whittaker's eyes narrowed.

"He had epilepsy," I explained. "I saw him have a seizure three years ago."

And as I stared at the headlines I recalled seeing Langley's eyes glaze over that day and go blank with shock, his muscles go limp and then seize with tension, his whole body quake with such force from the grand mal tremor that afterward he lacked the breath to tell me how to help him. He told me a few weeks later that he'd foresworn alcohol in the belief that the bottle of wine he'd split with a friend at lunch that day had triggered the seizure. I'd never heard him speak with more conviction.

"Denial is a common response to these things," Whittaker said. "Especially for someone who just went through what you did." He straightened up. "I talked to the doctor myself, Tom. He said Peter had a BAC of point two zero."

"I'm not in denial," I said. "I know he—"

"There's nothing we can do to change the facts. As a historian you should know that."

I stood up and walked to the window. I watched a pair of chickadees peck at a discarded pizza crust. Behind them the concrete edifice of the residential towers seemed heavier and more sullen than usual.

I turned back to Whittaker. "But we can try to explain what happened. As a teacher you should know that."

Just then the phone rang. I knew from Whittaker's side of the conversation who was on the other end: "Martha, yes, I heard . . . It is a terrible tragedy . . . we all feel that way . . . Why don't you take a few days? Yes that's fine."

It was Professor Martha Radisson calling, who, as I knew only too well, hated Langley and more than once had tried to ruin his career. The sympathy she was raining down on Whittaker was no doubt false.

Whittaker said goodbye and hung up the phone. "Everyone's shook up about this, Tom, even Dr. Radisson." He exhaled. "There's another problem," he said. "We're short staffed. I need you to teach Langley's American Revolution course."

"I can't think about that now," I said, exasperated.

"I know it's tough, Flanagan. It's tough on all of us. But I don't have time to find someone else and the department doesn't have the money to hire an adjunct. Besides, Langley has been grooming you for this for what, two years before you took time off? It's time for you to step up and show us that he was right in pulling you away from her."

I didn't answer.

Whittaker looked at his watch and said, "Cancel class this week. Monday's a holiday. Start teaching next Wednesday. Stop by if you need anything. And Flanagan, you are ready."

I ASCENDED THE STAIRS to the teaching assistant office suite and sat down. I took my Bible from my backpack, and surrendered myself to the ritual that had become my coping mechanism since I was first hit by personal tragedy four months before. I closed my eyes, opened the book and pressed my index finger to the page. That day, as on so many days past, the passage I pointed to put into words the feelings that were tearing away at my heart. From Psalm 13 I read:

> *How long, O LORD, will you forget me forever?*
> *How long will you hide your face from me?*
> *How long must I wrestle with my thoughts*
> *   and every day have sorrow in my heart?*
> *How long will my enemy triumph over me?*
> *Look on me and answer, O LORD, my God.*

Give light to my eyes or I will sleep in death;
my enemy will say "I have overcome him,"
and my foes will rejoice when I fall.

I'd been contemplating the psalm for about a half hour, not crying, but feeling the pressure of grief down into my bowels, when I heard a knock on the outer office door. I turned around and saw in the doorway an attractive, well-dressed woman with a leather coat folded in her arms. The black hair that fell down over her shoulders partly obscured a gold chain and cross that hung around her neck. At her feet were a small suitcase and shopping bag.

"I can come back if you're on your way out," she said.

I didn't understand until I looked down and saw that I was still wearing my coat and scarf. "No, it's OK. I'm just getting in," I said.

"Your glasses don't fog up?" she asked while scrutinizing me with her green eyes. "I bought contacts just last week because I couldn't stand wiping off my glasses every time I walked into a building. No one warned me that New York would be this cold."

"Can I help you?" I asked.

"I'm here to see Professor Langley," she said. She turned around and read the name card on the door. "You must be Tom Flanagan."

"Langley's teaching assistant. Well, I *was* his TA until this morning. Now I'm his replacement."

She stepped forward. "Replacement?"

I stood up. "Professor Langley was in a car accident last night. He died early this morning."

She tightened her lips into a pout. "I don't believe you," she said.

On the floor behind her was the copy of the newspaper that the building janitor always slipped under the door as a gift to the teaching assistants. Excusing myself as I moved past her, I reached around the shopping bag and suitcase, picked up the paper and unfolded it.

"Look here," I said.

But instead of taking the paper she moved her eyes towards me and then to the window. "My name is Julianne Radisson," she said.

I set down the paper and didn't comprehend her at first because my mind was back on the alcohol issue. Then it registered. "As in Martha Radisson?" I asked.

"Martha's my aunt," she said. "I'm the daughter of Harold's sister."

"Why were you looking for Langley?" I asked, instinctively suspicious of anyone related to Langley's rival. *Ex*-rival.

"I wanted to take Dr. Langley's course on the American Revolution. Since you're his replacement I still want to take it."

"You're a student here?"

"No. And I may or may not matriculate. For now, I'm here to take the course." Her eyes flitted again. "That's all I want is to take the course."

"Why?" I asked.

I watched her gaze become steady again. "For the same reason most students take it. To learn about the American Revolution."

That got me angry. "The room is full," I said. "You'll have to sign a waiting list with the others."

Julianne Radisson was offended. "I don't have to sign a list. I'm the niece of Harold and Martha Radisson."

"The room is full," I said with more conviction. "At least ten students have already signed the waiting list. Being Martha and Harold Radisson's niece does not get you preference."

She moved towards me in what a psychology student would call an invasion of personal space. I backed up only a step before stumbling into a chair and losing my balance.

But Julianne reached under my left arm and stabilized me, despite being a foot shorter than me and having no leverage. She moved her face a few inches from mine, her eyes burning now like copper flames.

"You should consider it a compliment that I still want to take the course even though it's you, TA, and not Professor Langley, the expert, who's teaching it." I could smell the peppermint mouthwash on her breath as she spoke. "And if you still decide not to let me in, I'll get permission from the department chair." She let go of me, tapped my chest with her forefinger, and stepped back. "See you in class."

She spun around on one leg, grabbed her shopping bag and suitcase with a swoop of her arm, and walked out of the room.

"Sign the list!" I shouted at her back.

LATER THAT EVENING, after a long day of thinking about Langley and looking over his notes for the course, I took a bus to a favorite local pub called 'The 357,' owned by a family friend named Louie Fratello. Louie had worked with my uncle Jack in the construction business until his knees went out after too much climbing ladders and crouching on roofs. He went into the tavern business, and connected his past and present lives by displaying behind the bar a collection of framed eight-by-ten photographs of the best houses he and my uncle had renovated or built.

Louie took a break from adding up receipts and poured me a pint of Genesee Twelve Horse. "My condolences, Tommy," he said with a frown and a shake of his head. "This is not what you need right now."

For a moment I thought he was talking about the beer, then he topped off the pint and placed it on the bar.

"Are you sure you're up to it? Going back to school?" he asked.

"I have to finish my degree sometime. Besides, I've been offered my first teaching assignment."

"Congratulations."

"It's Langley's American Revolution course," I said.

"Make every lecture an elegy," Louie suggested.

I smiled. "You bet I will."

Louie returned to his bookkeeping, and I made my way to the back of the room where two graduate school friends, Mindy McDonnell and Jens Erlenmeyer, were sitting.

"We were just talking about you," Mindy said. She smiled, and I took my time admiring the flecks of blue in her eyes that looked like sapphires embedded in granite.

I tapped my right ear. "I knew it," I said.

"It's about Walsh's grade," she added.

I groaned and sat down.

"He gave her a C plus," Jens said with conspiratorial solemnity. "We're going to file a grievance."

"We?"

"GOSH."

"Who?"

Jens took a puff from a freshly lit cigarette, and his face turned a shade closer to the red button down shirt he wore. "The Graduate Organization of Students of History," he said.

"Catchy," I said. "But it doesn't mean a thing to me."

"Alexa Ortiz and I started the group last semester," Jens said. He reached into his duffel bag and produced a sheet of paper. "Here."

It was the GOSH charter, a manifesto really that described the university faculty as "the servants of the students, whose duty it is to provide for us the programs we deem necessary to our professional education and development." It ended with a call to arms: "petitions and, if necessary, strikes to make our demands heard."

I handed the charter back to Jens. "What does this have to do with me?"

"I can't have this blemish on my transcript," Mindy said. "I'll never get into Harvard or Yale with a C plus in my major." She looked my way. "I need you to testify to the committee that Walsh was out to get me."

"I wasn't even in your class," I said. "I was in Florida all last semester."

"But you know Walsh."

"Did anyone else read your paper?" I asked.

"Rebecca Moreland from Art History. She said I deserved an A."

I shook my head. "She's just an adjunct, though. Lower than us on the faculty food chain. What exactly were Walsh's comments?"

"That I didn't spend enough time investigating the—how did he put it—the gender ideology of Thomas Gainsborough's paintings."

"Walsh thinks *The Blue Boy* was transgendered," Jens said. Mindy smiled.

"I'm teaching Langley's course," I said.

Mindy's smile faded. Jens' face lit up. "Political Protest?" he asked.

"American Revolution," I said to his disappointment. "FPP was canceled after the Bucci incident."

"Congratulations," Mindy said. "You're off the chain gang."

"Thanks. But you know that teaching makes it tough for me to help you. I don't want to piss anyone off, especially Whittaker." I remembered our conversation earlier that morning and wondered where my loyalties should lie.

"GOSH will be there for you, too," Jens said.

"I don't want GOSH there for me," I said.

"A rugged individualist," Jens said.

"An independent thinker," I countered.

Mindy took my hand. "Then think about helping me," she said. "Please."

AN HOUR OR SO LATER, after Jens left the bar with a group of German friends, Mindy asked me if I was doing all right.

"I had a cold last week, but I'm over it," I said.

Mindy frowned. "About Langley."

"I guess I'm OK," I said unconvincingly. "Although I wish someone would have a memorial service."

"Langley was an atheist," she reminded me.

"Memorial services are for the living," I said. "I for one need the closure."

"Is there anyone to talk to about it? Did Langley have family?"

"I think he was an only child," I said.

"Talk to the university chaplain, Tom. Maybe he can help you."

"I will," I said, then hesitated. "I'm also bothered about the drinking."

"I know something about that," she said after a moment of consideration.

"What?" I asked, puzzled.

"How well did you know him?"

"Pretty well, I thought. We went to lunch a few times each semester, and he took me to a Mets game once. What's up?"

Mindy tapped her foot nervously. "I wasn't going to tell you this."

"Tell me what?"

"Late last semester, while you were in Florida, Alexa Ortiz filed charges of professional misconduct against him."

I moved my chair closer. "What happened?" I asked.

"You didn't hear this from me. Understand?"

"Don't get cryptic, Mindy," I said, getting angry with her evasiveness.

She lifted up her glass of wine and set it back down. "Alexa caught him drunk on the job."

"What?!" The students at an adjacent table looked my way. I leaned forward and spoke softly. "What are you saying?"

"Alexa was his TA last semester, filling in for you. She

went to his office one evening in the middle of December
to get some advice on grading final papers. Langley was
bombed. He was slurring his speech. He made a pass at
her." Mindy paused. "Evidently, Langley told her to do the
best she could, then stumbled and fell over as he tried to
put his arm around her waist."

"Or so says Alexa Ortiz."

"Alexa didn't say anything, Tom. That's why I don't want
you to say anything." Mindy ran her fingers through her
hair. "Martha Radisson told me about it yesterday afternoon. She asked me if I'd ever had any problems with
Langley. I had no idea what type of problems she was talking about until she told me about Alexa. Now Langley's
gone, and I'm still not sure if I know what Martha's talking
about."

"Martha Radisson again," I said.

"Again?"

"I met her niece this morning."

"Long black hair? Expensive clothes?"

"Julianne," I said. "She wanted to take my course."

"Did you let her in?"

"No."

"Why not?"

"I think Martha wants her to keep an eye on me."

Mindy waited for more, then asked, "Why?"

"Do you know about her feud with Langley?"

"Only that they didn't like each other."

"In 1987 Radisson was denied tenure, due in large part to
Langley's sway on the Faculty Review Committee. But a
year later, tapping her husband's influence, she beat out
Langley for the directorship of the new Center for the Study
of American Revolutionary Culture and History."

"How does this concern you?"

"Martha Radisson was my advisor when I was a freshman. She put much effort into steering me in the right direction, which for her meant towards her and away from

Langley. And my indirect relationship with her goes even further back. My father used to run a newspaper, on the northern fringe of Harold Radisson's congressional district. In 1978 my dad helped deliver the votes that got Harold elected." I sat back. "When I matriculated into college Martha introduced herself as Harold's wife and said that she fully expected me to follow my father's political footsteps. She wasn't too happy when I refused to join the Young Democrat Society. She was outright furious when I chose Langley over her as my advisor during my junior year."

"I didn't know that," Mindy said.

"I know Langley didn't drink," I said. I was starting to believe that by repeating those words, I could make fact what everyone else seemed to believe was false.

Mindy finished her wine. "Did you know that Langley was supposed to become department chair next semester?"

"He didn't tell me that."

"There was talk among the grad students that Radisson was going to block his appointment."

"It seems it wasn't just talk."

"Right." She hesitated. "This chain of events explains a lot, Tom. First the Bucci affair. Then Dr. Radisson and Alexa file the charges, blocking Langley's appointment. Then he gets drunk and crashes his car . . . "

I moved forward again, almost falling off the chair, and tried to keep my voice down. "You're implying that Langley killed himself? You really believe that?"

Just then a train of students entered the bar, letting in with them a blast of cold air that hit the back of my neck and set my hair on end.

Mindy shivered too and looked at me with nervous eyes. "I don't know what to believe," she said.

Chapter Two

What dearer privilege, indeed,
than to do as our Sires have done;
To follow in the paths they proved,
to finish as they have begun;
To give to our children, undefiled,
all that our fathers won?

—Ausburn Tower, public oration, 1879

I SLEPT LITTLE THAT NIGHT. My upstairs neighbors were playing loud music for much of it, but nine years of apartment
living had inured me to such annoyances. What kept me
awake were the images that appeared the moment I closed
my eyes, as if on a projection screen, and the thoughts that
accompanied them like subtitles in a foreign language film.

Langley appeared first, his hair black and thin and
combed straight back, his loose skin hanging from his bony
frame, his blue eyes gleaming behind a pair of low prescrip-
tion bifocals. There he was, my mentor, calling from the
grave but unable to tell me how he got there, disgraced by
the means of his death but unable to defend his own name
and reputation. How well did I know him? Mindy's question
appeared as a caption superimposed upon the frozen picture of his likeness. As both image and words flashed across
my brain, my only answer was that I knew him well enough
to believe neither the rumors about nor accusations against
him.

I wasn't so self-assured when the other image, Mindy's, appeared and brushed aside that of Langley. We had been friends for two years, sharing both intellectual interests and hobbies, and had narrowly avoided the dissolution of that friendship after we briefly became lovers last April. At first our romance was a welcome and agreed upon tonic for the melancholia that afflicts many in upstate New York when nature belies the calendar and winter weather continues deep into spring. But it came undone when spring finally arrived, and with it the end of the semester. Mindy set off on a summer internship to England. I resented her for it. Grief and jealousy germinated and grew in my heart and choked off any real feeling of love I might have had for Mindy. Without warning I went on a steady diet of saltine crackers and boilermakers, and within a few days became as unpleasant as a field full of poison ivy and burdock.

Then came the deaths of my parents and younger brother in a Labor Day boating accident in the Thousand Islands. I walled myself off completely, and refused Mindy's consolations. On the day of the funeral I received a note from her:

> *I can't help you if you won't help yourself, Tom, and I can't carry your pain. I'm going into hiding, but not far away, and only in places where you know you can find me.*

The next day I drove to Florida to work the fall and early winter with my uncle.

The more I thought about my own decisive role in our breakup the more angry I became. The time we had spent together was magical: sharing ice cream in the student union, taking long walks along the river despite the cold May drizzle, making love in her bed and in mine and once in the shower of the women's dressing room at the university gymnasium.

Hindsight is always twenty-twenty, but we are still able to look back on our pasts through whatever color lenses we choose. The mistake I made in driving Mindy away can only be viewed darkly.

LATER THAT MORNING I was in the graduate student lounge, reading for the course and watching The Weather Channel, when Jens Erlenmeyer sat down on an adjacent couch and pulled from his duffel bag a bacon, egg and cheese sandwich that sold for a dollar fifty in the student union.

He jumped right in. "Mindy is concerned about you."

I kept my eyes on the book. "Hmm."

"She knows what you went through when your parents were killed. She knows your feelings about drinking and driving."

I closed the book and tossed it on the table. "The situations are completely different," I said. "My parents were killed by a drunk speed-boater. There was nothing I could do about that."

Jens took a bite of the sandwich. "There's something you can do about Langley?"

"I know he didn't drink."

"I'm not going to give unsolicited advice," Jens said to my relief. "I just thought you should know that Mindy cares."

"Thanks," I said.

Did I feel relief that the embers of our friendship were still burning? I didn't want to think about it anymore, so I picked up the remote control and switched to CNN.

But suddenly, as if he realized I'd somehow offended him by changing the channel, Jens leapt out of his chair, letting a piece of egg drop from his mouth onto the floor.

"It's Radisson," he explained.

I looked from Jens to the television and saw Harold Radisson speaking from behind a podium to a small audience that had gathered in the lobby of city hall. I turned up the volume.

". . . and so, with only a fraction of the love for America that Theodorick Crane displayed during the cold, hard winter of 1781, I call on my friends and colleagues in Washington and New York, in business, government, and higher education, to stand behind Patriot Village and pass on to posterity the pride and patriotism that animated the founders of our great nation. Let us keep the fires of liberty and freedom burning in the hearts of all Americans, old and young."

Radisson waved and thanked the cheering crowd as the video clip ended. The newscaster said that a model of Patriot Village was being unveiled that night and moved on to a story about life on Mars.

Jens finished his breakfast and wiped his hands on his red shirt. "You know about this, right?" he asked.

"Of course," I said. "Radisson's historical Disneyland. According to him it's going to revitalize the upstate economy."

And to his credit, the historical dimension of Patriot Village was just as important to the Congressman as the economic one. Specifically, Radisson invoked the name of his Revolutionary War ancestor, Theodorick Crane, whose image over the span of Radisson's political career had grown from that of a local war hero to that of a leading Founding Father. As Radisson explained it, Theodorick Crane's love for his country and courage in the face of danger would become evident as visitors followed his career; he would be the beacon to lead them to a new and heartfelt patriotism. Indeed, many of the park's attractions were to be modeled on Crane's military exploits. Visitors could fire replica cannon from a miniature Fort Stanwix, chase Indians through the woods and shoot at them with splatball guns shaped like muskets, charge Tories and dodge their water gun sprays in a reenactment of the Battle of Oriskany.

The ironic thing was that Peter Langley had played as significant a role in fashioning Theodorick Crane's image as my father had played in commencing the Congressman's political career. In his unpublished dissertation on the diplomacy of the American Revolution in New York State, Langley cited Crane as an important early advocate of independence, one of the most accomplished soldiers in the northern theater, and a

prominent Republican Assemblyman in post-war New York
politics whose career was cut short by an assassin's knife.

"You should join our protest!" Jens shouted.

I shook my head and sat down. "No. Never. I already told
you this. No way."

"I'll treat you to a night out at Louie's."

"No, Jens. This new student organization I can understand. The Clinton Falls Crusaders are another story altogether."

"Why?"

"Do I have to remind you? Two years ago you released
cockroaches into the air ducts of one of the Knolls atomic
power labs. Last year a logger got his finger chopped off
when his saw hit a spike you'd put into a tree. Sorry. Those
aren't my tactics."

And Jens himself was no stranger to heavy handed protest,
whatever the cause. He once told me a story of how he and a
few friends had infiltrated and exposed a German right wing
group called the National Front. One day, during a rally celebrating Hitler's invasion of Russia, he and his friends doused
a Berlin street with gasoline and blocked the skinheads' line
of march with a wall of fire. When one of the skinheads
caught fire, the Nazis retaliated by overturning cars and
throwing hubcaps and crowbars at a larger group of socialists
who were protesting the rally. When the dust settled five
people were dead and a dozen injured.

Jens and his comrades got caught, but were turned loose
after identifying three skinheads who, two weeks earlier, had
murdered a family of Turkish immigrants. The bad news was
that the skinheads discovered one of his associate's true politics and stabbed the friend outside his mother's apartment.

Jens shrugged. "We do what we must. The only way to get
publicity in your country is to do something rash. Besides,
Tom, this is important. The Patriot Village people want to
build on the last known breeding ground in New York of the

Great Gray Owl, and one of the few remaining habitats for an increasingly rare species of tree frog.

"And you know about Radisson's deal with the mayor ..." Jens caught my look of incomprehension. "Radisson agreed to procure federal money for a trash incinerator on the east side of Clinton Falls in exchange for a waiver to fill in seventy five acres of wetland. It's a crooked and immoral political deal, Tom."

"Too bad you weren't around when your countrymen started cutting down the Black Forest," I said.

"I do what I can, as we all should. Harold Radisson calls Patriot Village economic development and speaks of preserving America's national heritage. What we really need to do is halt environmental destruction and preserve our natural heritage." Jens turned away. "Did you know that Dr. Langley supported us?" he asked quietly.

"In what way?"

"In opposing Patriot Village. He argued that the land in question was already a historical landmark for the herbs and other plants that grow there and were used by early settlers for medicinal purposes. He proposed the land be made into an historical nature area supported jointly by public money and donations. He gave a speech on the subject at December's NYPIRG conference. It was quite a—what is the word?—a bombshell. Will you join me?"

I sighed, angry at Jens for pulling out the Langley card, yet without the energy to argue any further. "I want dinner and drinks. And I'm not carrying a placard."

Jens thanked me and shook my hand. "Welcome to the revolution," he said.

THE PROTEST WAS UNDERWAY when I arrived at city hall. There were about twenty-five demonstrators, mostly students, and each had at least one placard displaying slogans like "woods are for owls, not theme parks" and "we don't want your history/let the frogs and owls be." Ten city policemen stood between the Crusaders and the fifty or so people who had gathered to view the unveiling.

"Who's that guy?" Jens asked as he moved next to me, pointing to a tall man in an expensive suit who was talking and laughing with a group of other important looking people.

"H. Paul Gass," I said. "Harold Radisson's number one financial backer. My father used to know him."

And there were other people I recognized: the mayor, the university president, real estate developers, Harold Radisson himself. I saw the Congressman walk through a doorway at the back of the room and then saw him escort Martha, who wore a hat too large and formal for the occasion, to her seat at the right of the model.

Then the Congressman walked to the lectern and remained standing as the others sat down behind him. A spotlight positioned on a balcony illuminated his narrow face and forehead and shined on his neatly combed brown hair. He was tall, although it was hard to tell how tall from my vantage point, and his suit fit perfectly over his lithe body. The crowd quieted and turned to face him as he began to speak.

"History tells us that a people without history is a people without a soul. The virtue and glory of our forefathers may seem light years away in these times of uncertainty and confusion, but we can, through our monuments to memory, re-animate the heroes of ages past. That is the goal of Patriot Village, within whose stockade the past will indeed come alive. Families will talk to heroes of old. Cheer them on as they fight once more that never ending battle of freedom against tyranny, good against evil. Join them as they return home to their wives and children to carry on their lives under the twin banners of freedom and virtue that they defied death to defend. And this will be no spectator sport, for in the end, man, woman, and child will be humbled by the glory of our history, convinced that the American way is the best way, and compelled to carry out their own obligations in the continuing fight for liberty and freedom.

"Theodorick Crane and hundreds like him made the ultimate sacrifice so that their fellow Americans could enjoy their liberty and freedom. With the help of Patriot Village his legacy and that of his compatriots will live on."

The Crusaders began to chant their slogans as a television cameraman turned on his machine and walked our way. I found Jens and tried to position myself between him and the camera. I could no longer concentrate on Radisson's voice.

I moved around to my right, saw Martha Radisson's hat, and saw a couple rows behind her the unmistakable profile of Louie Fratello. I wished I wasn't there.

Then the audience cheered and cameras clicked. I saw the NewsCenter 9 cameraman walking along the model. I couldn't see much from my position at the rear of the crowd, so I continued moving to my right.

Suddenly there was a loud crash, then another, and a bitter smelling smoke moved across the room like a swift blue fog. A moment later water from the sprinkler system rained down upon everyone in the room. The police officers ran towards the Crusaders while a few people from the audience approached the model. Everyone near the stage was coughing.

Then one of the officers dashed by me from left to right, grabbed Jens, and forced him to the floor. I heard Harold Radisson calling for calm above the din of the crowd, then, through the crowd, saw him move to where his wife and Louie were standing. I turned and ran towards the officer who had pinned Jens to the ground.

"Let him go!" I shouted, taking care not to touch the cop.

"Step back, sir." The command was crisply and coolly issued.

"He didn't do anything." Behind me two other officers were struggling to retain a large man with a ponytail.

"I repeat: step back. Or you're under arrest."

No sooner did he say the words than I felt my arms being grabbed from behind. I had no time to pull away before a set of handcuffs was clapped on my wrists. The officer who cuffed me began reading my rights. She told me that I was under arrest for inciting a riot, disturbing the peace, destroying public property, and assaulting a police officer. I didn't resist.

As she led me towards the stairs I saw Harold Radisson kneeling over his fallen wife and the wet face of Louie Fratello staring at me with a look of disbelief and disgust.

LOUIE BAILED ME OUT a few minutes after midnight with a check for two hundred dollars. He had collected my coat, watch, and wallet, and handed me the latter two as we walked out of the police station. We were both silent, I too ashamed to speak, even to inquire about Jens, and Louie communicating with a silent scowl that was worth a thousand admonitions. Although I was still wet from the sprinklers and began shivering the instant we stepped outside, I didn't ask for my coat.

"What the hell's going on, Tommy?" Louie asked while unlocking the driver door of his black pickup. He got in before I could reply and opened the passenger door only after loosening his tie, starting the truck, and letting it idle for a moment. He tossed the coat onto my lap as I buckled up. His eyes were like ice.

"I went with Jens Erlenmeyer. He'd been pestering me to join a demonstration and I finally agreed." I reached down to turn up the heat and was thrown back into my seat when Louie hit the gas. "For God's sake, Louie, I didn't do anything. I was an innocent bystander."

"Were you now? Try telling that to the police. They think either you or your friend threw the bomb."

"Bomb?" I said. "I don't know anything about a bomb. Is that where the smoke came from?" Louie nodded. "I was there as a peaceful demonstrator, Louie. The worst thing I did was yell at a cop to leave Jens alone. I didn't so much as touch him. Or the woman who handcuffed me." I automatically rubbed my wrists.

"You say you didn't do it. There's an officer who suspects that you or one of your Crusader friends did. Your word alone won't beat his."

"What happened, anyway?"

"One of your Crusaders threw an incendiary of some sort into the model. Martha Radisson jumped back from it and fell to the floor. Her arms and legs were burned and bruised pretty bad, she cut her head open, and I think she sprained her ankle."

We were silent for a moment until it occurred to me that I hadn't even asked myself why Louie was at the unveiling. "What were you doing there?"

"I'm contracting the construction of the new Patriot Village buildings."

"How'd you land that?" I asked to a man who seemed very satisfied to be out of the construction business.

"Your uncle and I renovated Harold Radisson's house for one. And I have some friends on the financial end of it. It's a good job, Tommy. I don't want to lose it because Charlie Flanagan's son is hanging around a bunch of terrorists."

"They're environmental activists," I said a bit too wisely.

Louie glared my way, took his right hand off the wheel, and pointed a finger of warning. "They're not the sort of people you should be associating with."

I got out of the truck and stood for a moment holding the door. "You helped me last year when I needed help," I said. "I appreciate that. But that does not give you the right to tell me how to live my life."

With a fierce look on his face he reached over and shut the passenger door. Then he pulled onto Monroe Avenue with snow, salt, and gravel spraying from beneath the truck's tires.

MORE THAN ANYTHING ELSE I needed a shower. I took a long, extremely hot one, standing there for at least fifteen minutes as water cascaded down my face and back, at once painful and refreshing. I was hungry, but after drying off and putting

on a pair of sweat pants and a tee shirt, I was hit by an over-
whelming desire to sleep. I went into the kitchen, poured myself a glass of water, and, at quarter past one, headed for the
bedroom.

But before I got there I was interrupted by a loud knock
on the door.

"Who is it?" I yelled, exasperated.

"Jens Erlenmeyer. I think I owe you something."

I considered not opening the door, but did so anyway. Jens
was standing there with a serious look on his face, holding a
twelve pack of Beck's and a lemon. I let him in and closed the
door.

He took off his coat. "I promised you wouldn't regret it."

"It's late Jens, and I'm exhausted."

"I won't stay long," he said. "At least let me warm up."

He sliced the lemon, opened two beers, put a wedge of
lemon in each bottle and handed one to me. He put the other
ten bottles in the refrigerator. I sat down on the couch and
set the beer on an end table.

"The police think I threw the incendiary," Jens said.
"You've heard it was an incendiary?"

"Louie Fratello told me," I said, and took a swallow of
beer. "Why you?"

"Someone in the crowd shouted that it was the man in
red."

"You won't get much sympathy from me," I said, although
I could feel my anger dissipating.

"I swear I didn't do it. After hearing a loud noise, I turned
to my right and saw a man pointing an officer in my direction. He looked directly at me and walked away."

"He was probably there to defend the frogs and owls," I
said.

"He was not a Crusader," Jens insisted. "I know everyone
in the group by face and name."

"You think he threw the incendiary?"

"I don't know."

"What did he look like?"

"Short and rotund. He had a long scarf on under a tan coat. He wore a brown fedora, so I did not get a good view of his face. I did see he had a mustache." He finished his beer and went to the refrigerator. "Another for you?"

"No thanks," I said.

Jens gulped his beer and then asked, "Why were the police there? They've been absent from other, more high profile demonstrations."

"Someone must have tipped them off," I said. "Someone who knew there was going to be a protest."

Jens looked into the refrigerator, contemplating a third beer. Then he shut it. "There was a television camera there, right?"

"NewsCenter 9. You're thinking they might have the mystery man on tape?"

"Exactly."

"I have a friend in the AV department. Maybe he has friends at Channel 9."

"Get it," Jens said.

He grabbed his coat and walked to the door, but stopped short of it and hesitated. "You know, part of me is grateful that this happened." He leaned up against the door as I waited for an explanation. "We may be able to use this to our advantage."

"Your advantage?" I said. "The only results are an injured woman, a smashed model, and a heap of fines. Maybe even assault charges against you."

"We need publicity," he said. "We have had none in two years. Once people begin reading about us in tomorrow's newspaper, there will be results. I just wish the bomber's methods hadn't been so crude."

"All for a few owls and frogs."

"It's about more than owls and frogs, Tom, at least for me. I must maintain a certain . . . how should I put it . . . sharpness. If I abandon the cause for a while I may abandon it forever."

"The cause." I shook my head. "Leave me out of it from now on."

Jens walked out the door without reply. He left the rest of the twelve pack, I assumed, by way of apology.

Chapter Three

Most American heroes of the Revolutionary period are by now two men, the actual man and the romantic image. Some are even three men — the actual man, the image, and the de-bunked remains.

—Esther Forbes, *Paul Revere and the World He Lived In*, 1942

THE NEXT MORNING I GOT IT from Whittaker.

"Let's talk," he said when I finally opened the TA office door after ignoring a dozen or so of his knocks.

I followed him down the stairs and into his office and sat across from his desk.

"I read about your escapades," he said, holding up Sunday morning's *Clarion*. "You'll be glad to know that Dr. Radisson only suffered a few scratches and burns and a sprained ankle. It could've been far worse."

"For her or for me?" I asked, warming up to the role of outlaw.

Whittaker seethed. "I don't care one way or the other about your politics," he said. "Just don't make the department look foolish. This"—he hit the newspaper with the back of his hand—"this will make us the laughingstock of the university."

"It was all a misunderstanding, really. I was there as a peaceful demonstrator. The police have even cleared my name since then."

"That's irrelevant. You were there. Your name is here."

He slapped the newspaper again. "In here are the only facts that matter."

"What do you want me to do?" I asked with no intention of doing anything.

"Keep your mouth shut. Plead the fifth. Let me handle the damage control."

"How?"

"I'll issue a press release saying your involvement in the demonstration was an isolated act of indiscretion, of bad judgment on your part. I'll mention the emotional turmoil you're in after your parents' and Langley's deaths. If we're lucky, the newspapers will print it. If we're very lucky, they'll print it somewhere more visible than page ten of the local section."

I stood up to leave.

"Remember, Flanagan, you aren't just a student anymore. Your actions reflect this department. Erlenmeyer can attend as many protests and throw as many bombs as he wants. You have to watch your step."

"I understand," I said, and started for the door.

"Do you, Flanagan?" Whittaker said, stopping me in my tracks. I turned to face him and caught his glare. "With Langley gone, Martha Radisson becomes your advisor. The department can't afford a foul-up on that score either."

The department's reputation, the department's best interests: was there anything else Whittaker cared about? I paused for a moment and watched him watch me.

"Didn't it hit minus twenty eight the other night?" I finally asked to Whittaker's initial puzzlement. "You know, on the night of Langley's accident?"

Whittaker rocked in his chair. "Go on."

"He lived in a brownstone on the east end of town. What was he doing out near Westcott Creek on a night that cold?"

"Driving," Whittaker said. I smiled ruefully and shook my head. Whittaker rose from his chair. "There's something you should know, Tom. Last week Peter asked me if I thought you were ready to teach. After that he told me how he'd amended his will to give his library to the department."

"And?"

"Frankly, I think he'd had enough of the world. I think the Bucci shooting did him in. The president thought so too. He agreed with Martha and me that, sadly, Peter was unfit to be department chair."

I took a long look at Whittaker and nodded. "I do understand," I said. "Very clearly."

ANOTHER LONG DAY of teaching preparation was followed by another night at The 357. After explaining again to Louie my non-involvement in the demonstration and apologizing for my rudeness after he'd bailed me out of jail, I chatted with other grad students about school, politics and sports. I had three pints of Twelve Horse in me and was about to call it a night when, talking politics with Jens, I felt a finger being thrust into my back.

I turned around and saw Julianne Radisson, a half-empty bottle of Zima in her hand. She wore black stockings underneath a tight black dress. She had her hair pulled back, exposing a pair of gold hoop earrings. She looked like she was on her way home from the opera.

"Hey, hey, TA. Like what you see?"

"You're a bit overdressed for Louie's," I said.

She gave a puff of laughter then raised her bottle towards Jens. "Who's this handsome Viking?"

"Jens Erlenmeyer at your service," he said as he bowed and kissed her hand.

"He's quite a gentleman," she said to me. "A good example for you to follow." She finished her drink and thrust the empty bottle against my chest. "Would you be so kind as to get me another?"

I took the bottle to the bar. Normally I would have refused her, but I was empty myself and felt a little guilty for having brushed her off on our first meeting.

"Some woman there, Tommy," Louie said as he approached.

"Julianne Radisson," I said. "Niece of your friend Harold."

"I thought so," he said with a nod.

"You know her?"

"She was living with the Radissons when your uncle and I renovated their house. I think she's in one of my pictures." Louie turned around and scanned the collection of eight-by-ten photographs he displayed behind the bar, but was too busy to look closely. "Back here somewhere. Anyway, watch your step around her. She looks like a man-eater."

"I can handle her," I said. "Just keep the back door open in case I have to toss her out."

"Or run," he added with a raised eyebrow.

I picked up the drinks and returned to find Jens and Julianne in an animated discussion.

"Let me get this straight," Julianne said. "After two hours of holding the class hostage, Bucci was tackled to the floor by three football players."

"Two of them were ROTC," Jens said. "They communicated with hand signals. Bucci shot one of them in the groin when they tackled him." Jens stopped talking when he saw me approach.

"Were you his TA for this?" Julianne asked.

"I was in Florida visiting my uncle," I said. "I saw it on the news."

"Randy Bucci was able to walk right into class with a shotgun? That doesn't make me feel safe taking your course, TA."

"He had it in a gym bag," I said. "He was registered for the course, unlike you, so there was no reason for Langley to be suspicious."

"I thought you weren't there?"

"Langley and I talked about it the day before he died."

Jens, who wanted the spotlight back, said, "Did you know Bucci asked to speak with your uncle Harold?"

"He did?" Julianne said.

Jens nodded, lit a cigarette, and offered it to Julianne. She took it. "Bucci said the government had implanted a microchip into his penis," Jens explained. "He said the Bureau of Alcohol, Tobacco and Firearms was controlling his brain."

"He actually used that as his defense," I said.

"Did the jury buy it?" Julianne asked.

"He was found guilty on fourteen counts of kidnapping and assault charges and sentenced to twenty-five years in prison," I said.

"Did anyone check?" asked Julianne.

"Check what?" said Jens.

"His penis. For the microchip."

Jens and I looked at each other and winced.

"Don't dismiss every crackpot," Julianne advised. "One or two out of the bunch is bound to be correct." She smiled and blew a puff of smoke right at me.

JENS AND I LOST HER in the crowd after that. Then, after a few minutes of talking about her, Jens decided to join his German friends and move on to another bar where a band called Sludge was playing. I told him I was going to finish my beer and go home to bed.

But as I drank the last swallow Julianne reappeared, with her leather coat on now, and asked if she could buy another round. She did, we sat down at a table near the jukebox, and after taking a sip of her Zima she made a few selections.

"How's your aunt?" I asked.

"Fine. She'll be back to work tomorrow."

"Does she know who did it?"

"No." Julianne smiled. "Maybe it was Jens Erlenmeyer?"

"Not according to him."

She nodded her head. "I know. He swore his innocence to me earlier, before our Randy Bucci discussion. To tell you the truth I couldn't care less if he tried to blow up some model. And like I said, Aunt Martha is fine. Uncle Harold, now he's a different story. He's pissed. He says he's invested too much political capital in Patriot Village to let the project be marred by a bunch of left-wing protesters."

"So what's the status of the investigation?"

Julianne shrugged her shoulders. "It's odd. Uncle Harold has requested that the investigation be suspended until they decide whether to press charges. He rants on against the Clinton Falls Crusaders, but he won't do anything about it."

Then she glanced at the jukebox and changed the subject. "Do you know 'West End Blues?'" she asked.

"I've seen it on the jukebox, but I don't think I've heard it."

"It's a Louis Armstrong tune. One of his best. Oh, here it is."

She stopped talking and sat up straight in her chair. She closed her eyes and drew in her bottom lip as she fingered along on air trumpet while slowly rocking from side to side. When the song ended I asked if she really played trumpet.

"I used to," she said. "The choice after high school was between trumpet or dance. I chose dance because it helps me stay in shape. I still have my trumpet, though. It was a gift from my father the day I left for college."

"Where'd you go to college?" I asked.

"Mills College in Oakland. But I'm transferring to NYU in the fall, which is another reason I came east." She looked up quickly. "But I don't want to talk about me. I want to talk about you. How's teaching?"

"It's great," I lied. "I love seeing the sparkle in my students' eyes as the themes of my lectures unfold."

She smiled slyly. "You're writing your dissertation?"

"Not yet. I'm scheduled to take my exam in May. I can write my dissertation when I pass the exam."

"Do you have a topic?"

I nodded.

She looked at me for a moment, waiting for an answer. "You're an odd one, Tom Flanagan. Most graduate students I know start bragging about their work before anyone has a chance to ask. Like they'll write bestsellers or something." Julianne sneered. I said nothing. "So what is your topic?"

"How veterans of the American Revolution responded to a revolutionary world."

She put her elbow on the table and her chin on her hand. "Really?"

"Yes. The men who fought in the American Revolution witnessed one of the greatest eras of upheaval in world history. It started with them, then spread to France, Ireland, England, Haiti, and South America. What I want to know is how these American veterans interpreted and reacted to what was going on around them."

"Fascinating," Julianne said.

"Thank you. I don't flaunt my academic interests because I know most people don't care."

"You must have some great stories. Do you have a favorite?"

"I have several," I said. "I like the misfits. Or, as you put it, the crackpots."

"Let's hear some stories," she said, sitting back in the chair and crossing her legs. "Lecture me."

So I told her about George Rogers Clark of Kentucky, the leading post-war general in the Ohio territory who fell out of favor with the government when he accepted a general's commission from the French with plans to conquer Spanish Louisiana. He was hounded by government officials for years before retiring to his farm and his whiskey bottle in 1810. I told her about another Clark, Elijah, from Georgia. For him the war never ended: he took on the Indians, Spanish and whoever else he deemed an enemy from 1775 to his death in battle in 1799. And like his unrelated namesake he took a commission in the French army in 1793. I mentioned other veterans who went into politics as either

Federalists or Republicans. I ran through a list of officers who had retired to their farms and commented on public issues from afar. And last but not least I mentioned Theodorick Crane, the wartime hero and postbellum friend of the people. But I didn't think it necessary to elaborate on his story.

"Some people think he's the biggest crackpot of all," Julianne said.

I didn't quite understand. "Because he went into politics?"

"Of course not," Julianne said with a wave of her hand. She looked at me with excited eyes. "Have you ever heard of Cornflower's ghost?"

"No."

"The story goes back to the winter of 1781 when Crane executed an Iroquois woman named Cornflower that he suspected of being a British spy. As Cornflower lay there dying she swore her revenge. And sure enough, later that year Crane's two daughters died of smallpox. The following year his wife died of pneumonia."

"Some curse," I said.

"That's nothing," Julianne said. "Nineteen years to the day after Crane executed her she came back and slit his throat. He was found dead in his bathtub the next day."

I paused for a moment and considered how ridiculous her story would sound to a professional historian. Why, then, did I not doubt her as much as I should have? I was a historian, however, and had an image, at least, to uphold.

"The history books say that Crane was assassinated by a political enemy," I said.

Julianne nodded. "I know. But this is the story I grew up hearing, especially on Halloween and on my birthday. My mother used to warn me that Cornflower's ghost would materialize and slit my throat if I was a bad girl."

"Some birthday present," I said. "Did you believe her?"

Julianne bit her lower lip and said something that sounded like, "Did or do?"

"What?" I asked.

She looked at me without expression and said nothing.

"Where did your mother get this tale?" I asked.

"From Uncle Harold, actually. He got it from a set of
notebooks belonging to Theodorick Crane's surviving son,
Joseph. The 'memoirs of Joseph Crane' he called them."

I didn't recall reading about these memoirs in Langley's
dissertation. "Are the memoirs of Joseph Crane published?"

"I have no idea."

"Have you read them?"

"No," she said quickly, almost exhaling the word. "But
that's why I wanted to take Dr. Langley's course."

I nodded. "To get the historical background."

"I still want to take it," she said.

I considered her for a moment. "I'm not an expert," I
said, "but I'll do what I can."

"You can help me understand the story," she said. Then
she lowered her head, gave me a coy look, and slipped me a
piece of paper with her phone number written on it. "And
understand myself."

Chapter Four

When your army entered the country of the Six Nations,
we called you Town Destroyer, and to this day when
that name is heard our women look behind them and
turn pale, and our children cling close to the necks of
their mothers.

—Oneida Chief Cornplanter, to George Washington, 1790

WHEN I GOT HOME THAT NIGHT I read the relevant sections of
Langley's dissertation. I found nothing unusual in it—nothing that confirmed Julianne's story, that is—except for an
admission that Theodorick Crane's murder was "mysterious
at best." Langley explained this in a footnote: A man named
John Coffey had been tried posthumously for the crime and
found guilty of murder. But there were discrepancies in
Joseph Crane's account of the trial, the only extant evidence. Without specifying what the discrepancies were
Langley called Joseph Crane's memoirs "an elusive, incomplete and unreliable source of evidence that sheds little light
on Theodorick Crane's life or death." That was it. There
was no mention at all of Cornflower, no mention of her execution, no mention, of course, of her ghost. Did the absence of corroboration negate Julianne's tale? I wanted to
think so, but couldn't dismiss it, or her, so lightly.

THE NEXT MORNING, another cold one, I saw Mindy in the
student union cafeteria.

"Having breakfast?" I asked.

"Not with a terrorist like you," she kidded.

"My treat," I said, "if you'll lend me an ear."

We went through the food line and sat back down. Mindy looked over my plate of eggs, sausage and corned beef hash and raised an eyebrow.

"Food, glorious food," I said after a silent grace.

"Talk quickly," she said. "Your heart might not outlast your meal."

I laughed. "I had a conversation with Julianne Radisson last night," I said.

Mindy stuck a fork in her cantaloupe. "Really."

"She told me quite a story," I said. And as I recounted Julianne's tale I saw a glint of jealousy in Mindy's eyes that turned to irritation and maybe suspicion. Whatever she was feeling she remained totally unconvinced.

When I finished Mindy shook her head. "You bought all that?"

"Of course not," I said defensively.

But Mindy saw right through my denial. "Refresh my memory on Theodorick Crane," she said. "Then I'll tell you a story."

"Well, Crane was for the Revolution from the start," I said, "for patriotic reasons, of course, but also because his neighbor and enemy, Guy Johnson, was a Tory. The specifics of their dispute aren't clear, but we know from Crane's petition for an officer's commission that Johnson or one of his agents tried to swindle a prime piece of land from Crane and his wife, Elizabeth. He got the commission in late 1776 and was made captain in the New York Thirty-second Militia Regiment. Elizabeth and the children moved to Albany that same year.

"He fought better than anyone those first few years of the war. He was wounded twice at Oriskany, once at Bemis Heights, and again during an expedition through Cherry Valley. The last was the worst: he was shot in the abdomen during a raid on a Tory and Iroquois outpost and according to all accounts was near death. But he not only made it back to camp, he also brought back with him an Iroquois scout whom he had captured on the banks of Schoharie Creek. I've hiked that country, Mindy. It's good hiking, but I couldn't imagine doing it with an injury and a captured prisoner.

"Anyway, Crane took a leave of absence and recovered on his farm before returning to action in August 1779 as a major in the New York Fifth Regiment on General Sullivan's expedition through western New York—"

"The one where the Americans burnt all the Iroquois food supplies."

"That's right. It was overshadowed by the southern campaigns that began a year later so not many people know about it. But to the Iroquois it was and remains an atrocity."

"What did Crane do in it?"

"He only rescued General Enoch Poor's brigade from certain destruction at the hands of Joseph Brandt's forces and captured a band of twenty-five Iroquois warriors on a reconnaissance mission. His actions earned him a promotion to colonel and the command of Fort Montgomery right here in Clinton Falls."

"I worked there as a tour guide the summer before I met you. Langley got me the job."

"So you know what Crane went through as commander. No provisions, no ammunition, no support at all from a government that had turned its attention to the southern theater of the war. Over a hundred people died there in the winter of 1781 alone."

"He resigned his commission because of that," Mindy said.

"And he went into politics despising the men who led the war effort. He battled against the eastern New York oligarchy and accused them of harboring aristocratic and royalist pretensions. He opposed the Constitution on the grounds that it was merely a tool of the new aristocrats to wrest power away from the people, and in the 1790s was one of the most outspoken Republicans in state government. But in February 1800 he was murdered by John Coffey, a Federalist who thought Crane would lead the Republicans to victory in the upcoming gubernatorial election. Or that's what historians think anyway."

"You think otherwise?" Mindy asked.

"There are discrepancies."

"Nothing's cut and dried," Mindy said, "but it's usually not that hard to distinguish between the roses and the weeds."

I took my last bite of corned beef hash. "What's your story?" I asked.

"My story is about a woman named Mary Strong. I did some research on her for Langley last semester."

"Fire away," I said.

"Mary Strong worked undercover for the Americans during the Revolution, smuggling documents from Fort Niagara to a contact she had in Schenectady. One of her stopovers was Fort Montgomery. One of her contacts there was Theodorick Crane. She died there in the winter of 1781, along with the others." Mindy took a sip of coffee and sat back. "Here's the reasonable explanation for Julianne's tale. Someone picked up on the Mary Strong story, changed her name to Cornflower, and turned her life into a ghost story suitable for one of the Radisson family cocktail parties."

"Was this information in STARCH?" I asked. Martha Radisson's Center for the Study of American Revolutionary Culture and History housed one of the most extensive collections of Revolutionary War papers in the United States, and its existence single-handedly put the University at Clinton Falls on the academic map. Mindy and I both had spent many hours there reading hundreds of dusty, brittle documents and scanning untold yards of celluloid microfiche and microfilm. Langley, who believed the directorship of the archive was rightfully his, wouldn't set a foot in the place.

"That's where I got it," Mindy said. "The STARCH index says that many of Crane's documents were destroyed when the old State Capitol burnt down. Deeds and titles, marriage licenses, birth certificates, that sort of stuff."

"Did any of the papers refer to Mary Strong as Cornflower?"

"Of course not."

"Did any of them mention the Sullivan Expedition?"

"Only casually."

"Are Joseph Crane's memoirs there?"

"They were destroyed in the fire, remember?"

"Why didn't Langley mention that in his dissertation?"

"I don't know."

"What did he say about your findings?"

"That they confirmed his suspicions."

"What suspicions?"

"That Mary Strong was a spy? That Mary Strong died of natural causes? That Mary Strong had nothing to do with the Radisson family ghost story that he'd once heard? He really didn't specify."

"That in itself is discrepancy enough," I said. "I want to know what Langley was hoping to find."

Mindy picked up a piece of melon then set it down. "Look, Tom, you have better things to do than obsess over Julianne's ghost story."

"Maybe what I need is a diversion," I said to Mindy's displeasure. I took a bite of sausage. "Jealous?"

"She knows you were Langley's TA. She knows he was interested in Theodorick Crane. All she's trying to do is see how much of a rise she can get out of you." Mindy paused and gave me a look of such genuine concern that on another occasion would've melted my heart. "Or worse, as you already suggested, she's keeping an eye on you for her aunt.

Be careful around her, Tom. She's a spoiled brat, nothing but trouble."

'And understand myself.' Julianne's words from the previous night came back to me right then, and despite Mindy's warnings I told myself that even spoiled brats deserve a chance.

BUT WHAT JENS TOLD ME later that morning planted the seed of suspicion in my mind, succeeding where Mindy had failed.

Mindy had gone to the library. I was still in the cafeteria, eating a doughnut now, when I saw him walk in the far entrance. When I shouted his name a student at a nearby table pointed me out to her friends and whispered something to them behind a shielding hand. I caught her eye, and made my hands like claws and growled at her.

"Do you have Julianne's phone number?" Jens asked when he sat down. There was the possibility of disappointment in his voice.

"I do, actually. But I'm not really interested in dating her."

Jens smiled. "Good. But I want it now because I saw her talking with the mystery man last night."

"When? Where?"

"After our Randy Bucci conversation. Heinrich and I were leaving Louie's and we saw her leaning into the driver side window of a silver Dodge with New Jersey plates. I knew it was him the moment I saw him. I'll never forget that brown fedora."

"Did he see you?"

"No. He was intent on what Julianne was saying."

"Which was?"

"We were across the street. I couldn't hear what she was saying, but she was certainly animated in saying it."

"You didn't go over there?"

"No. I decided I'd talk to Julianne first."

"Who do you think he is?" I asked.

"I have no idea."

AND TO WATER THE SEED, Martha Radisson called me to her office later that afternoon.

"To talk about my dissertation?" I asked innocently.

"That too, if you wish," was her enigmatic reply.

I exited Hammond Hall and saw Zachary Walsh on his way back to his office from class.

"Hello, Tom," he said.

I stared for a moment at his clothes: green pants, white shirt, a flower patterned vest and a red bow tie. His blond hair was tied back in a ponytail, except for a lovelock that dangled onto his left shoulder.

"Professor Walsh," I said.

"I'm glad Whittaker chose you to teach Langley's course."

"Thank you."

"Can we talk for a moment?"

"I can't right now. I'm on my way to see Dr. Radisson."

"Later, then," he said. "We'll talk later."

After delivering some paperwork to the registrar I ascended the stairs to the STARCH complex, which filled the third floor of the administration building. I'd always found it odd how eleven years ago the university president, who loved the view from the third floor, agreed to move his offices downstairs to make room for Martha Radisson and her research center. And what an archive it was, with oak bookshelves, filing cabinets and reading tables, a lush green carpet, and a naturally-lit computer room that was the envy of all visiting scholars.

I said hello to the secretary and walked down a long hallway, past a large work room, past the climate controlled document storage rooms, and into the anteroom of the director's office. She was at her desk reading *The New York*

Times and eating a pasta salad. I cleared my throat as I approached the door.

She lifted her head. "Come in, Mr. Flanagan, come in." She folded up the paper. "I was just reading a story on the Patriot Village project. It seems most city dwellers would love to have another destination for an upstate getaway, especially one that brings their nation's past alive again."

The final phrase, which Harold was fond of using, sounded odd coming from the mouth of a professional historian.

"I'm truly sorry about the other night," I said as I sat comfortably in one of two swivel chairs facing her desk. "I assure you that I had no intention of getting involved in a violent demonstration. Had I known how events would play out, I would've stayed home." A suitable olive branch, I thought.

She forced a smile. "I know, Mr. Flanagan. I hold no grudges towards either you or Mr. Erlenmeyer. As far as I'm concerned the incident is—" The telephone rang and interrupted her. For some reason I expected her to finish the sentence, no doubt as her husband would have finished it, with the words "ancient history."

She told the person on the other end that she'd "have to look for it" and slowly got out of her chair and hobbled over to a filing cabinet to her left. "I'll be right with you, Tom."

As she returned to her desk with a file I saw on the side of her head the bruises and small cuts she'd received at the unveiling two days before. She sat down and resumed the conversation, and rotated her chair to face the panoramic view of the university lawn, Monroe Avenue and the brown and white hills beyond. I stood up to examine a set of four paintings that hung on the wall to Martha's right.

They were portraits of American heroes, transported to the modern age, with the initials "MC" scrawled in the lower right hand corner of each painting. One painting was of George Washington, dressed in an olive green Army uni-

form covered with medals and other decorations. The sil-
houettes of a tank and a helicopter filled the background. In
another painting Alexander Hamilton sat in an overstuffed
office chair taking a momentary rest from the paperwork
piled on the desk in front of him. He wore a dark blue business suit and held in his hand a quill pen. Behind him was a
sign that resembled a baseball stadium scoreboard and read
'Death Toll: 40,000.' My favorite, though, was a painting of
Thomas Paine, who, bespectacled and wearing a tie-dyed
T-shirt, stood proudly in front of a burning building holding
a French tricolor in one hand and a Molotov cocktail in the
other. The fourth likeness, which I did not recognize, was
also clad in military uniform and escorted an allegorical
Liberty figure over a bridge that spanned the Atlantic
Ocean. I was standing in front of tie-dye Thomas Paine
when Martha Radisson hung up the telephone.

"I've often considered taking them down," she said. "I
have, in fact, done so once. They seem to belong here,
though, and here they'll stay."

"Who's MC?" I asked.

"I am."

I turned around to face her. "I think they're wonderful
paintings."

"Thank you, Mr. Flanagan. There are twelve of them in
the series. The 'Apostles of Liberty,' I called it. I've given
away all but these. My radicalism has cooled off some in the
twenty-five or so years since I painted them, but the core
beliefs are still there."

"I wasn't even considering their politics," I said. "I
simply think they're fine pieces of art. Take Thomas Paine. I
like the way his blue eyes and rosy cheeks are echoed in the
French tricolor. I like the way his shirt reminds me of
Rothko. And the reflection of the bottle and the French flag
in his eyeglasses makes it even more interesting." I walked
back next to Martha's desk, about thirty feet away. "From
here, forgetting that I'm looking at a picture of Thomas

Paine, all I see are perfectly situated swirls and waves of color. And form and color, when you get right down to it, are the most essential components of all good painting."

"Very impressive, Mr. Flanagan." She stood up and limped to the doorway. "But you're a better art critic than historian." Without turning around, she pointed to the adjacent picture of the man escorting Lady Liberty across the ocean. "This is Thomas Paine. The swirls and waves of color belong to Theodorick Crane."

I walked quickly towards her. She was smiling.

"I thought . . . " My sentence trailed off as I looked from one painting to the other and back again. There was a resemblance in the likenesses of the two revolutionaries, enough to mistake one for the other, but I had forgotten that one of Thomas Paine's many endeavors in life—the one that took him from America back to Europe and into the cauldron of the French Revolution—was that of bridge architect.

Martha returned to her desk. "Which brings me, in a roundabout sort of way, to the reason I asked you here in the first place. Please, Mr. Flanagan, sit down."

She shuffled a few papers, stuffed them in a drawer, and continued. "Julianne informed me of your discussion last Saturday night. I want you to know that she is a very disturbed girl with some serious emotional problems. She's been trying to get over them for years. She's tried psychiatry, faith healing, everything. Nothing seems to work."

"I'm sorry to hear that," I said as I sat down.

"Yes, well, the reason she's living with me is that I could no longer bear the thought of her being in California under the influence of her father. I hoped a change in location would at least begin the healing process."

"Has it?"

"She's been here only two weeks."

"How does this concern me?" I asked.

"Part of her problem is chronic insomnia brought on by

recurrent nightmares. Ever since your conversation with her the other night, she's been having the nightmares again."

"Nightmares?"

"She didn't tell you?"

"She told me quite a lot, but nothing about nightmares."

Martha glanced out the window before returning her gaze to me. "For fifteen years now, maybe more, Julianne has had a recurring dream that she is being killed by the ghost of the Indian woman, Cornflower. What wakes her up is the sensation of her own blood splashing onto her face. She woke up in hysterics at three o'clock this morning. I had to sedate her."

I grimaced. "What can I do to help?"

"Don't let her into your course. Don't meet her at Louie Fratello's bar. Don't acknowledge her existence, in fact. Forget you ever met her."

"That would be difficult," I said.

Martha sighed and sat back in her chair. "Let me put it differently, Tom. With Dr. Langley gone I'm the only one qualified to administer your exam and chair your dissertation committee. Do what I ask and you'll have no trouble."

"And if I don't do what you ask?"

"Then I apologize in advance for what might happen."

"That seems a bit extreme," I said. I suddenly felt detached from my body, as if I were listening to someone else speak the words. I counted to ten in an attempt to clear my head.

"Extreme measures are often the most effective ones, Mr. Flanagan. You must understand that whatever action I take is all for Julianne's benefit."

I decided to clarify something. "Did Theodorick Crane execute Mary Strong?"

"You mean Cornflower?" Martha said, and then added quickly, "No."

But she flinched when I said the name Mary Strong, which at least told me something.

I was up from the chair when Martha said, "Julianne begins seeing another psychiatrist tomorrow, which should help. She needs to sort this out with a doctor, though, not with you. This is all for Julianne's benefit, Mr. Flanagan. All for her. You may go now."

I didn't argue or dispute. I nodded, said goodbye, and, as I exited, focused my eyes on the swirls and waves of color that were Theodorick Crane.

"AND THEN SHE TOLD YOU to stay away from her?" Louie asked.

"Clear away," I affirmed.

It was six o'clock in the evening, and I had just finished telling Louie the whole set of tales, from Theodorick Crane's execution of Cornflower to the Radisson family ghost story to Julianne's neurosis to Martha's threat. Louie, like me, had a difficult time filtering out the probable truths.

"You're having a hell of a week," he said.

"I'm having a hell of a year. I should've stayed in Florida."

"You're an upstate boy," Louie said. "We need you here."

I smiled. "Thanks."

Louie scratched his head. "This is a tough call, Tommy. I figured that Julianne would bring trouble, but it sounds to me like her aunt might bring even more. Are you sure Mindy and Julianne are talking about the same woman?"

"Based on Martha's reaction, I'd have to say yes."

"And Theodorick himself. You're sure he was murdered by this John Coffey?"

"That's what Langley said. He's the expert."

"Julianne said someone wrote memoirs. Maybe they can clear a few things up."

"Langley said Joseph Crane's memoirs were 'elusive, incomplete, and unreliable.' Mindy says they were destroyed in a fire. Julianne says Harold Radisson has them."

Louie leaned forward and rested on his elbows. "I advise
you to proceed with caution, Tommy. Harold's nice face is a
façade."

"What do you mean?"

"Did I tell you how I first knew him?"

"You and Uncle Jack renovated his house."

"And we had a mutual acquaintance, besides your father.
When I was just starting out I worked for a guy named Julie
Fagioli. Julie had a younger brother Stefano who was with
Harold in Vietnam and who worked with us now and again
when he needed money. They called him 'The Stitch' because he allegedly asphyxiated this guy by sewing his nose
and mouth shut with fishing wire. He then buried him under three feet of gravel. The guy allegedly slept with Stevie's
girlfriend while he was overseas. Whether the story's true or
not I don't know, but Stevie took pride in the name."

"He still around?" I asked. I thought of Jens' conspiracy
theory and wondered if the man at the demonstration was
Stevie Fagioli. But why would a killer lower himself to the
level of a small time terrorist?

"Don't ask me," Louie said. "I haven't seen either him or
Julie in twenty years. Maybe Congressman Radisson took
him to Washington." Louie snickered at the thought. "My
point is that he's the type of guy that Harold sometimes
does business with. Loyal but stupid. And dangerous."

"Did my father know Stevie Fagioli?"

Louie waved his hand dismissively. "Your father lived on
the other side of Harold Radisson's fence, the public side.
Harold is very careful about not letting the flock on one
side cross over to the other."

"My father wasn't a sheep, Louie."

"Sorry, Tommy. Bad analogy."

I hesitated. "I wonder if my father knew about
Theodorick Crane."

"Do you have any of his back issues?"

"I read through them earlier today. He mentioned Crane

a few times, but only in the context of politics. I wonder if he knew the secret history of Theodorick Crane."

"That depends on what side of the fence Crane was on."

I laughed despite myself. "Louie!"

He raised a hand in apology and said, "What does Mindy think about all this? I assume you told her."

I took a long sip of coffee. "She thinks Julianne is playing mind games."

"Jealousy?"

"More than that. You know how maternal Mindy can get. She doesn't want to see me hurt."

"Appreciate those good intentions," Louie said as he began stocking a cooler below the bar with beer mugs. "Do you want to hear a story about Julianne Radisson?"

I said yes and refilled my coffee.

"It was at the Radisson house. What do they call it?"

"Crane's End." Which, I recalled as I said the words, was at the confluence of Westcott Creek and the Mohawk River, a hundred yards or so from where Langley's car went off the road.

"Right, Crane's End. Your uncle and I were putting the final touches on the roof one day in early September, I think. It was incredibly hot outside, I remember that much. Around two in the afternoon Harold and Martha stopped by to check things out. They had Julianne with them. Your uncle was talking with the Radissons, and I was up on the roof on the other side of the house, banging away. Suddenly I hear Julianne screaming from somewhere down below. I look around and see her on the bank of the river, having an absolute screaming fit. Boy could she belt it out! Then she falls in the water—splash!—just like that.

"I scurry down the ladder and run as fast as I could to the river. I remember thinking how odd it was that no one else had heard her. Your uncle Jack had always been hard of hearing, of course, but Harold and Martha? I don't know. Anyway, I found Julianne on her knees in about two feet of water, trying to get up from what looked like a pretty nasty fall. I carried her back to her aunt and uncle. She said she'd slipped on a rock while feeding bread to some ducks. I didn't tell them there wasn't a single duck in sight."

"Interesting," I said. "I wonder if she remembers."

"I didn't remember it until I found that picture I was looking for the other night." Louie handed me the photo as a dozen people entered the bar and sat at tables under the window. I examined it as he poured and served their pitchers of Bud.

It was a photo of Harold, Martha, Julianne, Louie, and my Uncle Jack standing in front of Crane's End, the Radisson's newly remodeled colonial. The house was freshly painted, the lawn neatly trimmed. I turned the picture over; "September 1983" was scribbled on the back.

It was odd seeing a young Julianne Radisson, just as it was strange seeing her in the same picture with, and holding the hand of, Louie Fratello. It struck me that neither had changed all that much during the intervening thirteen years.

Louie, then thirty-three, had hair that was less gray and a half inch or so longer, but it was still close cropped against his large, round head. His eyes were as narrow then as now, and the wrinkles around them and to the side of his small nose were evidence of the long hours he'd spent attaching roof shingles under the sun, a few feet closer to it than most of us were used to. His body had changed little: thick, hard muscle strained the fabric of his work shirt, his blue jeans fit tight around a set of powerful thighs. Louie was hardly skinny—in 1983 as in 1997 he hovered around two hundred and thirty pounds—but he had a fat measurement of something like four percent and a cholesterol count and blood pressure well below normal. He claimed he had never exercised a minute since playing high school football, staying fit through constant hard work and a diet limited to pasta, bread, tossed salads, red wine, and one sixteen ounce steak per week.

As for Julianne, everything she would become was evident in that picture: the mischievous smile, the luminous green eyes, the graceful posture, even the stunning, long black hair. She was, even then, a miniature version of who she was now. It took me a minute to notice that this precocious seven year old was holding in her left hand a copy of *Great Expectations*. She looked playful in the photo, holding Louie's hand, tickling it with one finger: I might have pegged her as a flirt even then.

But the pensiveness in her eyes betrayed something other than playfulness. I might have been reading the present into the past, but I saw in those eyes not the innocent curiosity of childhood, but rather the knowing wariness of someone whose experiences went well beyond a child's ken. I finished my coffee and prepared to go home, wondering how much she knew then, and how often before the summer of 1983 she had heard the story of Cornflower's ghost.

Chapter Five

In the bleak midwinter
Frosty wind made moan,
Earth stood hard as iron,
Water like stone;
Snow had fallen, snow on snow,
In the bleak midwinter,
Long ago.

—Christina Rosetti, "Mid-Winter," 1875

A WEEK CAME AND WENT, and the only thing besides the calendar that marked its passing was a shift in the weather from bad to worse. I awoke on Saturday to air that felt almost balmy—the day's high of twelve degrees was the first positive double-digit reading all year—but carried with it the heavy, moist foreboding of a winter storm that was gathering strength as it worked its way across the Great Lakes and into upstate New York. The storm hit the next day, and along with a series of less powerful but equally disruptive squalls that followed dropped a three day total of thirty-eight inches. We were the fortunate ones: the same storm system buried areas to the west and north under four to five feet of snow. It was an unkind storm that closed the university, blocked roads, killed cattle, trapped able bodied men and women inside their homes, and brought fear and panic and even death to the elderly and infirm.

Mindy and I walked to church together on Sunday, and

on Monday, the snow day, I called a friend at the AV department to ask about getting the NewsCenter 9 tape. The lectures I delivered on Wednesday and Friday were competent, but it was obvious to my students that I was a rookie and obvious to me that my mind was elsewhere.

Each day that week I sat at my desk, pencil in hand, intending to summarize what I knew about Theodorick Crane and Cornflower and arrive at some conclusions about their lives and deaths. But each day as I set to work I was hit by a malaise that froze my fingers and numbed my mind, the result, I knew, of something more than a case of the midwinter blues. My unease was partly explained by Langley's death, an event that brought back dark thoughts and feelings from my own past: contempt for an uncaring God, jealousy towards those who had not suffered loss, resentment towards a world that seemed to offer no consolation. I had experienced these feelings before, and knew from experience how to deal with them. Each day that week I also spent time reading and praying the Psalms, but as the week wore on even that activity failed to hold my attention.

The fact was that since my encounter with Martha Radisson I could not decide whether to pursue a two hundred year old mystery or heed her words of warning and get on with my own life. I knew that to defy her would be to commit professional suicide. I knew as a historian that tales of murder and ghost stories were best left to popular fiction and television docudramas. The Radisson family tale was, as Mindy had suggested, a good one to tell at a cocktail party, or maybe to a class of undergraduates if the going got especially rough, but it was not something a serious student of history should concern himself with. Mindy knew this all too well, and in her usual clear-headed way warned me again against becoming too enticed.

And had the dead mysteries of the past been my only enticement I would have abandoned and forgotten the matter like an adolescent fad. But the past was linked to my present

in the person of Julianne Radisson, the intriguing and increasingly intoxicating descendant of Theodorick Crane. It
was because of her that I was now obsessed with the story;
it was because of her that I could find no peace of mind.
Sometimes I regretted talking to Julianne that night at
Louie's; other times I unfairly blamed her for shifting the
burden of her history from her shoulders to mine. And having not seen her that week I was beginning to wonder
whether she was a flesh and blood human being or, like her
version of Cornflower, a phantom culled out of my own hy-
peractive imagination. I was obsessed indeed, almost to the
point of questioning my own good judgment—and even my
faith.

NOTHING HAPPENED to buttress my faith as we recovered
from the snowstorm, and what seemed at the time clarity of
mind came from an unexpected source, out of equally unexpected circumstances. Twice a year the department held an
informal wine and cheese gathering to celebrate the renewal
of academic life and set off the new semester. I expected a
small crowd this year because of the snow, and when I
walked into the basement of Hammond Hall at seven
o'clock Saturday evening, I was surprised to see the entire
history faculty and most of the graduate students present.
Mozart's *Eine Kleine Nachtmusik* played loudly over an old
sound system but was drowned out by the din of conversation and laughter.

"Tom!" Alexa Ortiz shouted from across the room just
as I was hanging up my coat.

I poured myself a glass of Merlot and joined her.

"I'd like you to serve as GOSH representative on the
Committee of Departmental Affairs," she said cheerfully.

"Why me?" I asked, wanting to talk to Mindy.

"Because you know the faculty well, because we want
you to be a part of our student community. I really think
you can do some good."

Alexa wore her hair tied up with a copper scarf that matched perfectly the color of her skin. Her thin face and well defined features—narrow blue eyes, long nose, and tightly drawn lips—contrasted with her plump body and gave her a striking, indeed beautiful, appearance. She stood with her ankles crossed, one hand on her hip, the other holding a half empty wine glass.

"I'm teaching," I said, searching for excuses. "That would be a conflict of interest."

"Do you have health insurance?"

"No."

"A pension plan?"

"No."

"Then you're still closer to us than you are to them."

"Why's it always us and them?" I said, starting to fume over what Mindy had told me about Alexa's accusations.

"I didn't choose sides," she said. "I just happen to be on the oppressed side."

"I'll think it over, Alexa. I'll let you know next week."

She was relentless. "I need to know now, Tom. The first meeting's on Monday."

"I'll be in touch," I said curtly.

"Why not agree to it now? There's no real time commitment and it'll certainly look good on your résumé."

"And help out the comrades, right?" I wanted Langley's advice, and thinking his name set me off. "You know, Alexa, I'm surprised you had the courage to ask me."

"What are you talking about?"

"The charges against Langley."

She set her wine glass on a nearby table and looked perplexed that I had brought Langley into the conversation. "He's not the issue here, Tom."

"He is the issue, Alexa. He's the only issue. I don't know what you and Dr. Radisson are up to, but you aren't going to get away with it."

Now she was completely lost. "Get away with what?" she

asked. When I didn't respond she blew a puff of air and shook her head. "Tom, I have no idea what you're talking about."

"Langley might not have considered us professional equals, Alexa, but at least he treated us like human beings. That's no reason to issue false accusations against the man."

"False accusations? What are you talking about?"

Her surprise surprised me. "What happened that night you went to see him?" I asked.

"What night?"

"In December."

"What?"

"You told Doctor Radisson he'd been drinking. She filed professional misconduct charges."

Alexa's mouth tightened and she looked down. "He's gone, Tom. Let him rest in peace."

"What happened that night?" I demanded.

Alexa hesitated for a moment, then bit her lip and shook her head. "He was standing at the window. He looked gaunt, haggard, even more so than usual. His eyes were like glass, Tom, and he was slurring his words. I can't believe what he said . . ." Alexa slapped her palm on the table, looked around, and continued in a near whisper. "He told me he'd always considered me one of his most promising students, but that I'd sold out to Dr. Radisson. He became belligerent. I was very upset by this time, frightened. I had to get out of there. As I started to leave he grabbed hold of me and nearly knocked me down. I had no idea what his problem was. I balanced myself against a bookcase to keep on my feet and knocked an old volume of Francis Parkman off the shelf. With that Langley told me to get out of his office. I asked him if he needed help, but he demanded that I leave."

Alexa stepped back and looked at me with sad and angry eyes. "I told Dr. Radisson about it the next morning because I was concerned. She questioned me for an hour. She said there'd have to be an investigation despite my reassurances that nothing had happened. That was late last year. That was the last I heard of it."

Mindy saw us from across the room and walked our way. "Is everything OK?" she asked.

I glared at Mindy, confused and angry, my eyes not able to focus. "I was just saying how ironic it is that everyone's having a good time drinking wine while the best teacher the university ever had lies in a fucking casket with charges of professional misconduct hanging over his head." I was talking louder than I should have, at a moment when the conversation and music had quieted, and a few heads, including Martha Radisson's, turned my way.

"You need help," Alexa said.

I told her to go to hell and walked away.

Mindy followed me to the TA suite. I tried to wipe my face and eyes before she could see that I was crying.

"What was that all about?" She asked.

"Alexa said she has nothing to do with the charges," I said. "Martha Radisson concocted the whole thing."

"You promised not to mention that!"

My eyes, still wet, shot up to meet hers. "How could I not mention it, Mindy? How?"

Mindy looked down. "I'm sorry, Tom. I don't know what else to say."

"What she described to me sounds like a minor seizure. Did you know that Langley had epilepsy?"

Mindy shook her head.

I moved over to the window and watched the snow start to fall again flake by flake. "Alexa asked me to sit on the committee," I said. "Will you tell her that I'll do it? If she still wants me to."

"Yes," Mindy said. "Thank you." She handed me my coat. "You should go home, Tom."

"I need a drink. I'm going to Louie's."

Mindy said that she'd call me on Sunday evening and that

her grievance was being reviewed sometime next week.

With a forced smile I told her I'd be there for her. I promised myself to forget about Julianne and Martha Radisson and concentrate on helping my friend.

BUT ON MY WAY OUT of the building I heard Zachary Walsh call my name from behind.

"Good show in there," he said. "People around here are a bit too flippant about Peter's death for my tastes."

"Thanks." I pushed the handicap access button and walked out the door. Walsh hurried to catch up and just made it through as the door began to close. I walked faster.

"Especially his old friend Martha Radisson," Walsh said.

That stopped me. "What do you want?" I asked, looking straight at him.

"I was hoping we could talk."

"About what?"

Walsh smiled. "A mutual concern."

I turned and resumed walking. "I'm going to Louie's."

"I've heard some delicious things about that place. I'll give you a ride."

The bar was crowded when we got there. After five minutes of standing just inside the door Walsh and I made our way to a table being vacated by a group of students. As I moved around the table to a chair under the neon-lit window I saw Julianne and Jens talking at the far end of the bar, as close as two people could be yet still have room to breath. I set my coat on a chair. Walsh placed his on top of mine.

He took a sip of Chardonnay. "Not bad. What's your libation of choice?"

"Twelve Horse."

"Sorry?"

"Genesee Twelve Horse. It's made in Rochester."

"I should think you're too sophisticated for Genesee beer."

"I've got family there. It's genetic." I noticed I was nervously tapping my foot and said, "I assume you want to talk about something other than beer."

"Indeed I do." He sat back and crossed his legs. "As you know, Mindy McDonnell has filed a grievance against me for the grade I assigned her last semester. Since I'm up for tenure this year the Dean of Graduate Studies has strongly advised me to settle the matter before her office officially addresses it. I did my part by offering Mindy a B. She refused to drop the grievance."

I guessed at where Walsh was heading. "You want me to persuade her to drop it."

The way Walsh thrust his nose into the air when he laughed reminded me of a dolphin at play. "That would be impossible." he said. "I want you to submit a deposition to the review committee supporting my grading policy."

"What?"

"You're a straight A student. You were just elected student representative. You receive a lot of sympathy around here with the tragedies you've been through. Anything you say will more than outweigh Mindy's complaint."

"I've already promised to help Mindy any way I can," I said with obvious resentment.

"What I'm proposing is that we exchange favors. You do this for me and I'll reciprocate."

I laughed. "Dr. Walsh, there's not a favor in the world I'd betray Mindy for."

"Even if it involves important information about Doctors Langley and Radisson?"

I stood up and grabbed my coat, knocking Walsh's onto the floor. "I won't betray Mindy," I said with a certainty that wasn't yet strong enough to stand on its own two feet. "And I won't spend my time gossiping with you about a man I respected and admired."

Walsh calmly picked up his coat and brushed off a few peanut shells that had clung to its bottom hem. He returned it to the chair. "Let me put it differently, Tom. I overheard your conversation with Martha Radisson last week. All of it. If you refuse my offer, I'll have no alternative but to inform her that you've been holding secret trysts with her niece Julianne." He looked over his shoulder then up at me. "She's the young girl speaking with Jens Erlenmeyer, correct? Dr. Radisson has ruined the life of more than one nosy graduate assistant, you know."

"You overheard our conversation?" I said, wanting to punch him.

"Yes, quite by accident. After I saw you I realized I had some papers to deliver to Martha. I got to her door just as you finished your analysis of her painting. So I waited outside and listened. It was quite fascinating, especially when she threatened you." He snickered. "Do you want to hear about Peter and Martha?"

I sat back down, hungry now for Walsh's bait and feeling hooked. "What is it?"

Walsh smiled with satisfaction. "It's not commonly known that Peter and Martha attended graduate school together in the early seventies. Martha Radisson was going by her maiden name then, and her affiliation with SUNY was never acknowledged because she completed her Ph. D. elsewhere. At Rutgers, I believe, but I'm not certain. Nevertheless, they knew each other and were very good friends. They were involved in student politics, in fact, along with a friend of theirs named Albert Hartman. Do you know him?"

"Of course," I said. Hartman's book on the American Navy and the war of 1812 had been a runner-up for the 1974 Whitbeck Prize and was now considered a classic for its frank depiction of sailor life at sea and on shore. But he was a one hit wonder, I recalled: soon after writing the book he left academia and hasn't been heard from since.

"Do you know his story?"

"No."

Walsh shifted in his seat, gleeful at the opportunity to

gossip. "Well, then. The three of them were best friends in their years at SUNY Albany, all history majors and all student activists. By 1970, in fact, Peter and Albert were two of the most influential students on campus. They ran a series of what they called political history seminars in which they discussed different aspects of radical politics, preparing themselves for the coming revolution. One of their seminars in May of 1970, right after the Kent State massacre, was interrupted by some Weathermen who were dissatisfied with the moderation of Peter and Albert's leadership. A scuffle ensued that left Albert injured and, worse, left both him and Peter discredited in the eyes of the other students.

"That was only the beginning. A few years later a corpse was unearthed in ground underneath what is now a gymnasium and was identified as one of the students who had led the coup against Peter and Albert. Police inquiries revealed that the student had been killed in a hit-and-run accident, and that his body had been buried by the driver in an attempt to conceal the crime. It took the police about a week to identify the driver as none other than Albert Hartman." Walsh snickered. "Apparently he got his revenge."

"And he went into hiding before the police could catch him," I said. Then I asked, "Why is this story important?"

"Because Peter was convinced that Martha reported Albert Hartman to the police."

"What?"

"He blamed Martha for the destruction of his best friend's academic career. That's how their ongoing dispute began."

"How do you know this?"

Walsh stood up suddenly. "Campus gossip, Tom. Open your ears from time to time and you'll hear quite a bit of it. Your conversation with Martha Radisson is a case in point." He put on his coat and scarf and flipped his lovelock over his shoulder. "I fulfilled my end of the bargain. I expect you to fulfill yours."

AFTER WALSH LEFT I MOVED to the front end of the bar and
sat there alone, drinking and thinking. I needed to talk, but
Mindy was probably at home, Louie was too busy to talk,
and even though Jens and Julianne were only a few yards
away they seemed too absorbed in each other to bother.

But by eleven thirty I had four pints worth of irascibility
and false courage in me and I didn't care whether I was interrupting anything. I walked over to where Julianne and
Jens were sitting.

Julianne was smiling, and judging from her glazed eyes
and the contents of the ashtray was matching Jens drink for
drink and smoke for smoke. She and Jens stopped talking
and set down their drinks when they saw me crossing the
bar.

"Let's go," I said.

Jens extinguished his cigarette. "I hope you're not talking
to either of us."

I avoided his eyes. "Come on, Julianne."

She looked at me and scowled, but said nothing.

"Leave her alone, Tom," said Jens.

"We need to talk right now," I said. "It's private." Jens
and I were drunk and were talking past one another and,
like drunks tend to do, were arguing over decisions that
were someone else's to make.

"Leave her alone, Tom," Jens repeated.

Ignoring Jens I grabbed Julianne's wrist as she moved the
bottle of Zima to her mouth. She started to return the
bottle to the bar, but after I let go of her wrist she dumped
its contents down my shirt. Then she threw the empty
bottle to the floor, where it smashed at my feet and got
Louie's attention.

Julianne stood up and yanked her coat from the back of
Jens' chair. Her eyes were so wide and bright with anger
that I thought I could see my reflection in them. "What if I
don't want to talk? And if I don't want to go? Or even stay?
God, you two can be jerks."

She walked towards the door and Jens started after her. I moved into his path but not quickly enough, and I was off balance when he shoved his elbow into my chest. I took hold of his arm, both to maintain my own balance and to keep him from continuing on. He pulled away from my grasp, took two steps back, and swung his left fist at my face. I ducked under it, but right into an uppercut that ricocheted off my chest and into my chin and knocked me backwards into a Biology student who I knew from an intramural bowling league.

Jens moved towards me, fists clenched, ready to deliver another blow if I chose to continue. But Louie, who had seen his share of bar scuffles and knew how to distinguish between dangerous and harmless ones, had moved from behind the bar and stood between us, laughing.

"One week you two are getting thrown into jail together, the next you're throwing punches at each other. Do you want me to lock you in the back room so you can duke it out? Any of the rest of you want to pay five bucks a pop to see it?"

Jens was the first to smile, then I and everyone around us laughed.

Jens offered to buy me a beer, but I was embarrassed at having lost control of myself for the second time that night, and wanted nothing more than to get out of there. So I took a taxi home and went to bed.

BUT I WAS AWAKENED at five in the morning, while dreaming, by the thud of snowballs against the window. The dream was a strange one in which I walked outside one morning to the sight and smell of daffodils and blooming forsythia and the sound of peepers, and went to bed that same day with the trees shedding their brown and orange leaves and a cold autumn rain beating at my window. In my dream, the usual three months of summer in upstate New York lasted from about five minutes before noon until five minutes after.

The snowballs continued to hit. I looked out the window to see who was there, my eyes as foggy from alcohol and disturbed sleep as the windows were from the cold. Unable to see anything, I put on my coat and walked outside.

Julianne was standing there packing another snowball.

"What are you doing?" I asked.

"It's about time you got up" she said. "I've been trying to wake you for ten minutes." She missed me with the snowball then crossed her arms and rubbed them with her hands. "Can we go inside?"

Once in my living room Julianne took off her leather jacket and I placed a blanket around her shoulders. We sat down, she on the couch and me on a rocking chair facing her.

"Jens and I were having fun until you showed up. Do you always bring out the worst in people?"

"Don't make me out to be the bad guy, Julianne. Last week your aunt threatened to ruin my future if I didn't stop talking to you about Cornflower. Did she tell you that? And tonight another professor threatened to do the same thing if I don't take his side in a tenure dispute. I was more than justified in interrupting you guys."

"You were also drunk. And rude."

"I know. And for that I apologize," I said.

Julianne drew her knees up to her chin and pulled the blankets tight. She exhaled upward, blowing the hair off her forehead. "That night Professor Langley was in the accident..." She hesitated.

"Yes?"

"He was arguing with my aunt that night."

I moved forward in the chair. "About what?"

"About Theodorick Crane and a woman named Mary Strong."

My pulse quickened. "Known to your family as Cornflower," I said.

"Yes," Julianne confirmed.

"What did they say?"

"Profesor Langley wanted to know where Joseph Crane's memoirs were. He knew Aunt Martha had them and was certain that they told the truth about Crane's murder. He demanded to see them, and Aunt Martha refused. It sounded to me like they'd had this argument before."

"Was this at the house?"

"No. In Aunt Martha's office. I met Aunt Martha there to lend her my car. Her Saab needed a tune-up, and she needed to borrow my car. I heard them arguing as I approached her office, then listened for two or three minutes before walking in on them."

"And then?"

"Professor Langley left and I drove Aunt Martha home."

"Had you ever met Langley before?"

"No."

"Was he drunk?"

A look of surprise, then unease flashed across Julianne's face. "Drunk? I didn't think much of it then, but now that you mention it, well, yes. He did seem drunk."

"Damn," I said. I stood up and walked to the window, and thought about Mindy's suspicions and then about Julianne's credibility. "I called the registrar the other day, Julianne. You never signed up for my course."

Julianne paused for a moment, then sighed. "To be honest, I had no intention of taking the course, taught by Professor Langley or you. All I wanted was to talk to him about Theodorick Crane and Cornflower. Then I met you."

"Why Langley?"

"My father told me he might know something about Theodorick Crane's murder. He said Langley was the expert."

"How did your father know about that?"

"I don't know. He just knew."

"Is your aunt aware that you sought out Langley?"

"God, no. If she ever found out she'd ship me back to California express."

"She is suspicious," I said. "That much was obvious from the conversation I had with her. Did you plan on telling me your story when you came to Louie's that night?"

"No. Yes. I don't know. I thought I might, but I wasn't sure until you mentioned Theodorick Crane."

I walked to the couch and sat down beside her. "Last semester a friend of mine did some research for Langley on Mary Strong. She found out that this Mary Strong—Cornflower—died of natural causes in February 1781. Then you come to town hoping that Langley can tell you the truth about Crane's murder, which, of course, he can't. Now you tell me that Langley and your aunt were arguing about Theodorick Crane and Mary Strong on the night of his accident. Did you know he and your aunt were enemies? Do you know your aunt filed professional misconduct charges against Langley late last semester?"

Julianne slowly shook her head.

I continued. "I think Langley knew something about Theodorick Crane and Cornflower that your aunt didn't want him to publicize. I need to find out what Langley knew, Julianne. I need to know the truth."

"I want the truth too, Tom. I've had enough of taking everyone's word for it."

"Help me, then. Help me get Joseph Crane's memoirs."

She turned towards me, her eyes bright and wide and moving back and forth like tennis balls. A tear welled up in the left eye and run down her cheek, and I wondered despite myself whether it was real or for show.

"I don't know if I can," she said.

"Why not," I asked, almost whispering now, almost pleading too. "You said the other night you wanted to understand things."

Her mouth trembled. "Cornflower has been haunting my

family since Theodorick Crane executed her, Tom. She still is."

"What?"

"She's been haunting us, exacting her vengeance like she said she would. My mother's sister drowned in an auto accident. While my cousin was scattering her ashes on the Maine coast, she was knocked down by a wave and broke her neck. Two years ago my mother was electrocuted when her hair dryer fell into the tub while she was taking a bath." Julianne hesitated and wiped her eyes. "Cornflower was there on all three occasions."

"Julianne—" She cut me off with a raised hand.

"And now she's after me, Tom. I used to think I could protect myself from her by hiding out in California. But I realized I was wrong when she killed my mother and resumed haunting me. I came here to find her and face her, Tom. I came here to free myself from her before she destroys me."

"She's haunting you?"

"Yes. I saw her for the first time when I was a child. I can't remember how old I was. I was staying at Crane's End for the summer and was down by the river throwing rocks. I was watching one of them skip across the water when I saw her on the other bank, standing in front of a large outcrop. She wore an old gray dress and no shoes. Her hair was black and longer than mine, and seemed to move even though there was no wind blowing. She just stood there and looked at me for the longest time. Then she motioned for me to cross the river. I became hypnotized. I waded in. But I got no more than three feet when I slipped and fell. Before I could stand up I was pulled out of the water by a man working on Crane's End. I looked up and Cornflower was gone."

"That was Louie Fratello," I said.

"I know. I've seen Cornflower a few times since then. Once more at Crane's End a few years later, again when my mother brought me out here for my grandmother's funeral. And more recently in my dreams, a few weeks before I met you."

I stood up and blacked out for a moment, whether because I moved too quickly or because I finally knew the full weight of Julianne's albatross I do not know. I took a step back and stumbled. Then Julianne stood up, the blanket slipping off her shoulders, and allowed me to place my hand around her arm and on her wrist.

Her touch was soft and trusting as she looked into my eyes and said, "I'm frightened, Tom."

As my vision cleared I guided her back to the couch. She leaned her head against my shoulder, a few strands of her damp hair resting on my neck, and I put the blanket and then my arm around her. I sat beside her for hours, holding her close as the soft glow of dawn worked its way across the albescence of the accumulating winter snow. Julianne was afraid: I recalled Louie's story and shuddered.

Chapter Six

I have seen the Mississippi River. That is muddy water. I have seen the St. Lawrence River. That is crystal water.

—John Burns, letter to the *London Daily Mail*, 1943

JULIANNE HAD AN ALBATROSS, Langley deserved the truth, and I knew that the two problems were linked. But how? The answer, it seemed, lay in Martha Radisson, aunt and self-proclaimed guardian to the one, colleague and long-time enemy of the other. She was the lodestone between them, and now I too found myself caught in the field she projected. As I sat in the microfilm room of the library after church on Sunday morning I thought back to simpler days, not long past, when my parents and brother were alive, when the name Julianne Radisson meant nothing to me, when the war between Professors Langley and Radisson was nothing more than fodder for graduate student gossip on a weekend night at Louie's.

But the information I found in the library only strengthened my resolve. I left the film in the machine and returned home, where Julianne was still asleep on my couch.

"Want to join me on a road trip?" I said.

"Today? Where?" she asked groggily.

"To the Thousand Islands. There's someone there who should be able to enlighten us."

"Thousand Islands? Like the salad dressing? Where are the Thousand Islands?"

"On the Saint Lawrence River," I said, "a hundred miles north."

And at last count there were over seventeen hundred islands, ranging in size from under an acre to over thirty square miles, spread out between Lake Ontario and Chippewa Bay, split territorially between the United States and Canada. I had spent the summers of my youth there, reading, fishing, playing gin rummy and racing my father out to the floating dock he'd anchored a hundred feet from shore. As a teenager I would join my father and uncle on their diving expeditions to investigate any one of a number of old shipwrecks that littered the river bottom. They were vacations full of hamburgers and orange Kool Aid and beaches and laughter, memories made bittersweet by the death of my parents and brother in the water I had grown to love.

"What time is it?" Julianne asked with a yawn.

"Eleven thirty. Let's leave by noon."

JULIANNE SLEPT on the ride along New York's spine, and I passed the time reciting verses of Psalm 42: "Put your hope in God, for I will yet praise Him, my Savior and my God." We ran into foul weather just south of Boonville, where the snow, already piled up five feet high along the road's shoulder, began to fall like confetti dropped from the ceiling at a New Year's Eve party. I woke Julianne and explained how just a few weeks ago the Tug Hill Plateau to our west had received seventy-seven inches of snow in less than twenty-four hours.

She sat up in the seat, yawned, and said, "One day?"

"I think it was from six in the evening to six the next evening," I said. "But yeah, two turns of the clock."

"You mean we could slide off the road into one of these snow drifts and then get buried by another six feet trying to find our way back to civilization?"

"That wouldn't happen here," I said. "But it might if we were a bit farther west."

She glanced over at the speedometer. I was going thirty. "Slow down," she said.

"There's a town right up ahead. We can grab lunch or find a place to stay until the storm blows over."

"In twenty-four hours after six feet of snowfall," said Julianne. "We'll end up New York's answer to the Donner party, en route to the Thousand Islands."

She leaned her elbow against the door handle, propped her head against her open palm, and stared out the window. As we crossed the Boonville town line a few moments later Julianne saw the large welcome sign on a hillside to our right and said, "Boonville? We're entering a place called Boonville? Good God."

We entered the Adirondack Diner and sat down at the only vacant table, to the right of the door and under a large tinted window. After we ordered Julianne asked me why we were on our way north in the middle of winter.

"We're going to Wellesley Island, specifically, to see a man named Ben Fries."

"Means nothing to me."

"Let me tell you what I know about him," I said. "For thirty years my parents owned a cottage on Wellesley Island. Each summer we'd vacation there, my mother and brother and me all the time, and my father when he wasn't working. Relatives from all over would join us, some for a whole month, some for a week or two. The place was always packed with people, and it was the most fun I'd ever had. Then every couple of years a cousin would graduate or an aunt or uncle would pass away, and there'd be one fewer of us at the cottage. Finally there was just me, my parents, and my younger brother. I stopped spending whole summers there in '84 when I took a job as a camp counselor.

"One thing I'll never forget was this guy down the road named Benjamin Fries, spelled F-R-I-E-S but pronounced freeze. I didn't know that at first and called him Mr. French Fries. He became something of a local celebrity because of an environmental group called 'Preserve the Islands' that he founded in the mid-seventies when an oil barge ran aground and spilled 300,000 gallons of crude into the river."

I paused as the waitress refilled our cups of coffee. "Ben Fries and my father were good friends. They played cards together and organized the Bicentennial celebration. My father even helped now and again with Preserve the Islands. But then they had a falling out over pesticide use on a golf course or something. I don't remember the details. Anyway, one day in the summer of 1980 I took the eighty-seven cents change I had in my pocket to Ben Fries' house and offered it to him as a donation. And who drove by as I was standing at Ben's door? My father, returning from a golf match. He scooped me up with one arm, tossed me in the back seat of the car, and paddled my rear end sore when we got back to the cottage.

"But after that I was more eager than ever to see Ben. I'd sneak over to his house and we'd fish off his dock, and if either of us saw my father coming I'd jump into the river and hold out underneath the dock until he was gone. Every year from 1980 to '84 I'd spend as much time fishing with Ben as I did doing anything else. The last time I paid him a visit was in 1985, my senior year of high school."

The waitress brought our lunch, a fried cheese and to-mato sandwich for Julianne and a tuna melt for me.

"What's your point?" Julianne asked before she took her first bite.

"I saw Ben Fries again this morning."

She set the sandwich down and stopped chewing. "Where?"

"In back issues of the Albany *Times Union* from April 1975. His picture was at the head of each in a series of articles about a man named Albert Hartman."

"So Albert Hartman knew this Fries person in 1975?"

"Albert Hartman *is* this Fries person," I said. "It was one picture, one man. His hair was darker and he didn't have a beard in the photo, but I recognized him immediately."

"I don't understand," Julianne said. "Who was Albert Hartman?"

"A graduate student friend of Langley's and your aunt Martha. The three of them went to SUNY Albany together." I took a sip of coffee. "Julianne, do you know your aunt's maiden name?"

She didn't answer.

"Crane. As in Theodorick Crane." Julianne took another bite of her sandwich but didn't say a word. I continued. "After graduate school Hartman got a job teaching history at the University of Rochester. But he went into hiding when a warrant was issued for his arrest in the 1973 hit-and-run murder of another student named Garrett Hollister."

"And he resurfaced in the Thousand Islands," Julianne said with controlled excitement.

"As Ben Fries," I said. "As the man I knew as a kid."

MEMORY ENLARGES AND MAGNIFIES, even distorts to the point where the thing remembered seems somehow changed in its physical reality upon viewing it again. Such was the case with the American span of the Thousand Islands Bridge, which seemed magnificent by half since I had last seen it and nothing like the giant steel beam and cable monster that had frightened and astounded me as a child. Now, having become familiar with the Tappan Zee and George Washington bridges, I was unimpressed by the size of this one. Yet I realized as we ascended it that it still retained for me its magic as a carrier of people away from the turbulence of everyday life to a vacation land on the other side, to a paradise not yet lost where time could be put on hold for a week or two. On this trip, looking down at the partially frozen river and the snow covered evergreen islands below renewed my faith in God's ability to provide certain places that could heighten the spirit and renew the soul, whatever the season.

Julianne was moving her head from side to side, trying to take in the entire vista. We were the only vehicle on the northbound side of the bridge, so I slowed down to a crawl to facilitate her viewing. I smiled as she craned her neck and focused on a point at the distant horizon because it reminded me of a game we played as children in which the first family member to see a ship and say so would win a quarter from all the others.

This was no game, though, no excursion into a vacation wonderland. Rather than putting time on hold Julianne and I were taking a necessary step back in time, seeking answers from a man who had known Peter Langley and Martha Radisson and perhaps their secrets while living another life some twenty years before. And as we descended the bridge onto Wellesley Island I had a sinking feeling that if Ben Fries's present world was a paradise, it was about to be spoiled by a visit from his own ghost.

The river wasn't visible from the road on much of the west end of Wellesley Island. But as we entered the village of Thousand Islands Park the woods to our left opened up to reveal a commanding view of the seaway channel, Grennell Island, and the mainland hamlet of Fisher's Landing. I drove on autopilot, past the general store and tennis courts and boat launch, my hands knowing instinctively which turns to make. I pulled onto Seaway Drive and stopped the car.

"The second cottage from the end is mine," I said.

I gazed apprehensively upon its shuttered windows and bolted door. It had been mine for five months, yet I hadn't set foot in the place since I'd inherited it.

"It's gorgeous," Julianne said. "Smaller than I pictured it, but beautiful. Where did you fit so many people?"

"The size is deceiving from this angle. Hold on." I moved the car farther up the street and pointed back at the cottage. "Look there. See how it juts out over the river? And see the boathouse? There's sleeping quarters for six in there." I recalled with a smile how lucky we were as children to spend mischievous nights away from sleeping adults. I remembered too standing on the dock with my toy plastic tool belt, wanting to be a man like my father and uncle Jack as they repaired the boathouse roof. Both of them were large men, and I could still see their muscles straining from exertion and their skin glistening with sweat beneath the summer sun.

"Why is it closed up?" Julianne asked.

"I don't use it," I said.

"Does your family?"

"My parents and brother died in a boating accident on Labor Day," I said. I glanced at Julianne, who was watching me wide-eyed and turning pale. "See that small island with the red house on it? They were rounding that island in my parent's Lyman when a drunk speed-boater cut them off. My father tried to avoid him, but he flipped the boat and rammed it into the dock. The Coast Guard told me my parents and brother were killed instantly."

"I'm sorry," Julianne said.

"The speed-boater got away," I said as calmly as I could manage.

WE LEFT THE CAR where it was and walked the half mile to Ben Fries' bungalow, small, plain and well-situated at twenty or so yards from the river. There was a dark blue Ford pickup in the driveway. I presumed he was home.

But no one answered my knock, so I instructed Julianne to stay at the door and walked around the house, thinking he might be somewhere outside. As I rounded the southeast corner of the house a large chunk of wet snow fell at my feet, causing me to step back and gasp. I looked up and before being blinded by the sun saw Ben Fries standing on the roof, shovel in hand.

"You're trespassing, son. That's not a good idea with the homeowner in such an advantageous attack position." He had another shovel full of snow ready to let fly.

"I'm looking for Benjamin Fries," I said. "I have a donation for Preserve the Islands."

Ben knelt down and cautiously set the shovel on the slightly pitched roof. "Donation?" he said suspiciously. I figured he didn't receive many this time of year. "Give me a minute, I'll be right down. My ladder's on the other side of the house."

I walked over to meet him and saw to my left the dock where Ben and I had once fished, moved onshore now to protect it from the ice. When he stepped off the last rung of the ladder I extended my hand and smiled. "It's a donation of eighty-seven cents."

Ben looked puzzled for about three seconds and then parted his lips in a wide smile. "Tommy Flanagan!"

He took my hand and shook it vigorously. His graying hair and beard were thick. He was at least six foot four and straight as a board. The skin of his face was stretched taut and dry, like the bark of an oak tree around his eyes. I wondered whether it was worry or time that had done such work, and wanted more than ever to hear his story.

"Let's see," he continued, "you were the only one in your family brave or foolish enough to disobey your father and fish with me."

"And the only one in my family not to think you were a Cuban spy."

"You were wrong about that," he said with mock solemnity. Then he laughed. "Your mother sympathized with me, you know. She donated fifty dollars a year."

I didn't know.

Ben softened his grip and lowered his eyes. "I'm sorry about your parents and brother, Tom. That was a terrible thing."

"Thank you," was all I could say, remembering as I spoke that I hadn't seen Ben at the funeral.

After a moment Ben returned his gaze and said, "Your cousin does a fine job with the cottage for you. He was here last weekend, in fact, patching up a leak."

I took another long look at him, and the memories came flowing back.

"Let's go inside," he said finally. "You're not here to talk about the river. Inside and over coffee we'll see why you're two hundred miles from home on a cold February day."

WE FOLLOWED BEN'S LEAD and kept our shoes on as we stepped into the kitchen, a small room yet one nicely arranged and filled with sunshine. We removed our coats and laid them on a small table, and then he led us into a large living room, its ceiling stained yellow with decades of soot and wax. The braided rugs on the floor were worn out, yet soft and useful. One wall consisted of recessed bookshelves, another had in it a picture window that afforded a wide view of the river. A third wall was broken up by a steep stairway. Across the stairway was a fireplace, and inside it flickered an orange and yellow flame that warmed the entire room. Julianne took a seat on the sofa in front of the fireplace. I sat in a comfortably padded straight back chair in front of the bookshelves.

Ben returned to the kitchen after seating us. He brought back a tray of hot coffee, and gave us each a cup before sitting down across the room in a chair much like the one I was in. He crossed his legs.

"A proper introduction," he said, looking at Julianne. "I'm Ben Fries."

Julianne looked at me and then back at Ben. "Julianne Markbright," she said, flashing a fake smile.

What to say when Ben asked Julianne her name was something neither of us had thought of: revealing her identity most likely would mean revealing the reason for our visit. I appreciated her lie, but knew that the subject had to be broached sooner or later.

Better sooner, I decided, and said, "Her real name is Julianne Radisson. One thing we know about you is that your real name is Albert Hartman. And one thing you probably don't know about me is that I was Peter Langley's teaching assistant."

Benjamin Fries—for that's how I had always known him and will always remember him—straightened his legs as a flicker of surprise crossed his face. Then he smiled, and the tension that I felt enveloping the room vanished. "As long as you're not here to have me arrested," he said. "Remembering your father's opinion of me, Tom, that's what first came to mind. Langley and Radisson. It's been a long time since I've heard those names."

"I've been Dr. Langley's TA for two years," I said. "I have bad news about him, Ben. He was in an auto accident on the thirteenth of January. He died the following day. His doctor told me that he'd been drinking."

"My God," Ben said, his expression barren.

"It gets worse. I think Martha Radisson was somehow involved."

"How? Why?"

Julianne answered. "The evening of Langley's accident I overheard him and Aunt Martha arguing about Theodorick Crane and Cornflower. To find out about those two, Crane and Cornflower, is the reason we're here."

Ben Fries picked up his cup of coffee and took a long, slow sip. "Where should I begin," he said more to himself than to us. Then to Julianne, "You want to prove your aunt's innocence?"

Her face had turned pale, despite the heat of the fire, and she spoke in a slow, quiet voice. "I'm the one who wants to know about Theodorick Crane and Cornflower. I told Tom about them in the first place."

"Why?" asked Ben.

"To clarify a bothersome piece of family history," Julianne said.

"What history?" Ben asked.

"The ghost story. Cornflower's execution and Theodorick Crane's murder."

Ben stood up and turned towards the window. Just offshore a lone seagull sat on a chunk of ice that protruded up and out of the partially frozen river. Ben rubbed his temple as he stood there, and sighed loudly before speaking. "I'd forgotten about that story. I'd forgotten much about those days. But I remember now that we got a lot of mileage out of the joke after Martha told us about it."

"It's no joke," Julianne said curtly.

"I'm sorry," said Ben, sensing her anger and turning around. "You can certainly understand why budding historians like Peter and I snickered at talk of Cornflower coming back from the dead to slit her executioner's throat. And I tell you, what we knew for certain about Theodorick Crane's life is dramatic enough without the supernatural element. The ghost story seemed like unnecessary embellishment."

"So Martha told you about it and not Harold," I said, leading Ben forward.

"Yes. She discovered Crane's secret history while doing family research in Albany. That was in, let's see, 1970."

"Martha Crane," Julianne said uneasily. "I grew up hearing that Uncle Harold discovered Theodorick Crane's story."

Ben shook his head. "Harold was ignorant of all history until he realized he could use it for political capital, and even then it had little meaning to him beyond being a good story with which to lead off a speech. No, Harold knew nothing about Martha's family until she told him."

"But Uncle Harold says . . . Are he and Aunt Martha related?"

Ben turned to face Julianne. "They're distant cousins of

some degree, but, if I remember correctly, not through the Crane line. Your uncle Harold, how should I put it, adopted . . . no, grafted a few branches of Martha's family tree onto his own. He did it, as he did so many other things, to gain political capital."

"What do you mean by political capital?" I asked after unsuccessfully trying to interpret Julianne's blank expression.

"Harold felt the need for a revolutionary war ancestor whose virtues he could trumpet in campaign speeches in lieu of any real political program. He didn't have one of his own so he appropriated Martha's."

"With her consent?" I asked.

"With her encouragement," Ben said. "They devised the ruse together just after Martha first proposed stealing Theodorick Crane's papers."

"So she did steal them," I said excitedly.

"Not her alone, though," Ben explained. "We were all in on it. And we were simply carrying through what Hiram Crane had begun."

"We?" I said. "What do you mean 'we'? And who is Hiram Crane?"

"By we I mean Martha, Harold, Peter, and me. And by Hiram Crane I mean . . . " Ben saw my surprise at his answer to my first question and sighed. "Why don't I start from the beginning. We'll see then what answers I can provide."

Chapter Seven

Sometimes you do indeed need a Weather-
man to know which way the wind blows.

—Albert Hartman, student newsletter, 1970

"I'VE ALWAYS BEEN CONVINCED," said Ben, "that Peter and I became involved in the whole affair as a direct result of our failure within the student movement. You must understand this, so I'll go into some detail in telling you about our politics.

"We were both student activists, but of very different types. I was the organizer. In November 1966 I founded a campus chapter of Students for a Democratic Society. In April 1967 I led demonstrations against military recruiting on campus. In September I organized a Civil Rights Society in tandem with black students and a local AME church. Also that summer I initiated a campus SDS newsletter that had a first run of two hundred copies. In most of this work I followed in the footsteps of my father, a labor organizer in New York City.

"My most successful venture was a series of political history seminars that I started in October 1967. They were both pedagogy and propaganda, an outgrowth of a summer workshop on the history of activism I had attended at New York University. Each week we discussed issues and ideas of all sorts, but I tried to keep the focus on comparing and contrasting different modes of protest and revolt. We covered topics from Bacon's Rebellion to the American and French Revolutions to 1870 Paris to 1917 Russia to Second World War pacifism to the Cuban Revolution to the Civil Rights Movement. It was a mishmash, really, as we skipped from one period and place to another, letting the ideas flow freely. But we were serious about history and about the lessons we could learn from the past.

"Peter was the thinker of our group, the one who figured out exactly what those lessons were. He came from a working class family in Herkimer, New York, the first in his family to attend any school beyond Herkimer Community College. But he knew his history. He told me when we first met that from third grade on he'd read two books a week. It seemed to me that he had read everything written about American history from 1600 to 1820.

"When I met him in 1968 he had already formulated a clear vision of what he thought we should do. He saw in the rising tide of American protest before 1776 a model that our student movement could emulate. While other radicals, myself included, celebrated Castro and Guevera, Marx and Mao, Peter admired the Adamses, Jefferson, Hancock, and Paine. He believed that American students in the 1960s had nothing in common with Russian factory workers in 1917 or Chinese peasants in the 1920s or Cuban farmers in the 1950s. We couldn't truly sympathize with them, he said, because we didn't suffer under an economic tyranny that left us poor and underfed, screaming from the belly for change. Unable to understand the way the world's angry poor lived, there was no way we could understand their style of revolution.

"What we could understand was our own revolutionary tradition. Peter believed that Americans in 1968 had to be convinced that revolution was in their best interests, as Americans in 1776 had been convinced by the Adamses and Hancock and Paine. As John Adams had put it, the revolution had been won in the hearts and minds of the American colonists well before the war was won on the battlefield. That was the pre-revolution, the winning over of hearts and minds, and that to Peter was what students in 1968 should focus on. We should educate and mobilize rural communities and city neighborhoods, appropriate and modify the words and slogans of the Revolutionary era to attack the problems that we faced, offer the public a clear and coherent view of our political position, and show the people that we're not just a bunch of dope-smoking, brick-throwing, spoiled-brat hippies. All this would culminate, Peter believed, in the election of delegates to attend a constitutional convention in the summer of 1976.

"Finally, like me, Peter looked askance at violence. He believed that violence could only lead to factionalism within the movement and be counterproductive in that particular stage of revolution. Violence had its place in the revolution, just as it had in 1776. But first people had to be convinced that violence, on a large enough scale to be effective, was worth their while. Petitions, demonstrations, sit-ins, editorials, mostly against the slow sapping away of our freedoms and liberties by an ever more intrusive government: these were Peter's forms of protest."

Ben took a sip of coffee and continued. "The problem with his analysis, of course, was that the issues we faced were filled with such immediacy. There was a war going on, an evil war, that had to be stopped. There was racial injustice that had deep roots in the ideas and policies of the very men Peter admired. There were people living in poverty as bad as any Cuban peasant faced. I knew all along that Peter was a step or two behind in his radicalism, making arguments that would have sounded fine in 1962 but sounded outdated by 1968 and 1969. I know now that he was also a patriot who loved his country, something few of his contemporaries understood."

"When did Martha join your group?" I asked.

"In 1970," Ben said. "She, too, remained in upstate New

York to attend college. She came from Elmira, the daughter of wealthy parents who had inherited some of their money and had made the rest, a lot of it, in real estate. Her father had agreed to pay all her college expenses on the limiting condition that she attend a state university and major in business. But she loved history, and halfway through her sophomore year cajoled her father into allowing her to study the history of American business. She was beautiful, with long flaxen hair and gray-green eyes that always seemed to twinkle. I'll never forget the day she walked into the common room of our dorm and asked if she had found Al Hartman's seminar.

"She never spoke up in my seminars," Ben said, "but her mind absorbed like a sponge every word we said. A comment she made one day summed up her view of the movement. Peter and I were discussing the value of sound historical research when Martha chimed in about not wanting to be holed up in a dusty archive when the steamroller of change rolled through our country. I asked her what she meant, and she said that whatever changes were about to take place, from wherever on the political spectrum they originated, she would be one of the bulldozer's drivers."

"Was Uncle Harold part of your movement?" Julianne asked.

"Not exactly," Ben said. "We met him for the first time, in dramatic fashion, in May 1970. By that time the Weathermen had already disrupted our lives like a cyclone. They made their first appearance on campus in February 1970, and within a few weeks had convinced at least twenty of our followers that violence was the only pure path to revolution. Our seminars got more and more boisterous that semester. Peter and I more than once got shouted down. For awhile in April Peter dropped out of politics altogether and concentrated on his senior thesis, an analysis of the American Revolution in New York State. I held down the fort, which really meant refereeing between two increasingly hostile factions that seemed close to ripping each other's throats out.

"Then came Kent State. The reaction in Albany was typical with students taking to the streets with the frightening thought that if it could happen there it could happen here. The worst riots were on May fifth: bricks thrown through administration building windows, fires set in science labs, bomb scares, overturned cars. It was enough for the university president to cancel final exams. We didn't give up. Peter returned to action the day after Kent State, and together we tried to channel student anger into constructive protest and reform."

Ben shook his head. "No one, though, was thinking of anything other than destruction. Our misreading of the situation was disturbingly obvious as Peter and I entered the commons room on the night of May sixth. The room was packed with at least one hundred students that night, by far the largest gathering we ever had at a seminar. Martha Crane sat anxiously in the front row—anxiety, in fact, hung in the air. I looked to the side of the room and saw five Weathermen who everyone knew had participated in the worst riots at Columbia and in Newark. They had distributed a leaflet on campus the day before warning 'all pigs and piglets' that Armageddon was here.

"I pointed out our guests to Peter and kept a watchful eye on them as he began the seminar. He talked about how our job as a movement was to imbed the tragedy of Kent State into the nation's collective memory, just as colonial Americans had done with the Boston Massacre. He warned against the Left turning Kent State into a rallying cry for immediate violent action.

"Peter was no more than ten minutes into his talk when one of the Weathermen stepped forward and asked about revenge. Peter started to respond but was cut off by shouts from the audience. At that moment I realized that two of the Weathermen were in a course I had helped teach the previous semester, my first as a graduate student, and that one of them, Garrett Hollister, worked in the library. All five of them moved forward, saying that the time for talk was over and the time for bloodletting was at hand.

" 'Let's purge the fucking revolution,' Hollister said with fury. Recognizing me, he shouted how I'd sold out to the system. He showered me with invectives: 'Dr. Fuckface' and 'Professor Shithead' were two of the more civil ones. He moved around me and grabbed me from behind, then pulled out a knife and pressed it against my throat. He whispered in my ear that I'd 'fucking failed' him."

Ben hesitated as the memories came flowing back. "Peter stood in shock, immobilized as the other Weathermen surrounded him. One of them produced a gun, a pistol of some sort, and pointed it at Peter. Here we were, advocates of non-violence, totally over-matched by rage.

"I wondered what the crowd would do. They were silent and still, and that seemed strange to me. Why didn't anyone do anything? Had we lost that much influence? Then I looked at a couple of kids in the front row, and at Martha Crane, and saw in their eyes the unmistakable blankness of fear. I realized then that their insulation from the larger movement had resulted in incomprehension, that the safe path of protest upon which we had led them had prepared them for none of this. They simply didn't know how to respond.

"Then I saw someone press his way through the crowd to the front of the room. He stood there for a moment when he reached us, wearing his dress greens, a lieutenant in the United States Army. I was astonished. When Martha saw him she stood up and screamed 'get out of here Harold!'

"Harold Radisson walked up to the man holding the gun to Peter and said, 'Are you going to use it? If so, use it on me.' He gestured at his uniform. 'I'm the enemy. I'm the establishment. Use it on me.' The Weatherman looked at Harold, angry but worried, still directing the gun at Peter.

"Harold moved quickly. Looking into the Weatherman's eyes he lunged forward and grabbed the gun. Then he took a few steps back and aimed the gun at Hollister, who still had the knife to my throat. 'I've shot and killed NVA at longer range than this,' Harold said. 'They thought they could use the hostage trick too. Are you as willing as they were to die for a cause? If so, stay right where you are for five seconds. See what happens.'

"Harold didn't bother to count, but I certainly did. After three seconds Hollister shoved me forward into the crowd. I fell into Martha, tripped over a chair and bruised my ribs against the floor. Peter and Martha helped me up as Harold kept the gun moving back and forth between the Weathermen. He motioned for them to back up against the windows and for us to leave out the emergency exit in a corner of the room. We did, my chest in pain, my arms slung over Peter and Martha's shoulders. We got into my car and drove away. Garrett Hollister threw a rock at the car as we pulled away, but all it did was dent the roof."

"What was Harold Radisson doing there in the first place?" I asked a moment later.

"He wanted to gauge the opinions of the student population, he wanted to protect Martha from harm, and most of all, I think, he and Martha wanted to enlist Peter and me into their scheme."

"So they had something planned all along," I said. I looked at Julianne who was staring into the fire, and couldn't tell what she was feeling.

"They told us about their plan that night," Ben said. He took a sip of coffee. "Let's turn to Theodorick Crane and to his great-grandson, Hiram. Their stories should help you understand what Harold and Martha were up to.

"You know the basic outline of Theodorick's life as

presented in Peter's dissertation. He was the son of poor tenant farmers, settler in the Mohawk Valley, hero in the Revolutionary war, radical politician. But Hiram Crane knew more. In 1876, as secretary of the Elmira Centennial Committee, Hiram cataloged thousands of correspondence, wills, church records, diaries, newspapers, and all sorts of other documents, many of them penned by Theodorick Crane, some by Theodorick's son Joseph, a few by Cornflower. He discovered two things about his ancestor that few others knew. First, that Theodorick had executed a spy named Cornflower, also known as Mary Strong, while serving as commander of Fort Montgomery.

"He did execute Cornflower," I said.

"Yes. She was an American spy, an important one, until she became disillusioned with the American war effort after General Sullivan's 1779 expedition through central and western New York."

I nodded, remembering my recent conversation with Mindy on the subject. "The American army burned dozens of villages and food-stores," I said. "Some people thought the expedition was a failure because there were no major battles and because the Americans took no Iroquois prisoners. But Sullivan pretty much knocked the Iroquois out of the war."

"He also fomented dissension among the five Iroquois tribes," Ben said. "The Oneida, who'd been our allies from the beginning, split on whether to stay with us or join with the British."

I nodded again, thrilled as I moved within grasp of the answer to the historical puzzle. "Cornflower wanted a British alliance," I said.

"Yes. And when a neighboring Oneida village found out what she was up to they sent out a raiding party to burn down her village. That was in late January 1781. Cornflower and the surviving villagers fled, and were captured a few days later by Theodorick Crane's men. But the Americans had nowhere to put them, and Crane denied them entry to the already overcrowded Fort Montgomery. Within days most of the refugees died of exposure penned in just outside the fort's gates. But Cornflower met her end in a different way. When Crane found out she was among the refugees he ordered her execution. He pulled the trigger himself on February 11, 1781."

Without turning from the fire Julianne asked, "And who killed Theodorick Crane?"

Ben shifted in his seat and breathed deeply before speaking. "That answer relates to the second secret Hiram Crane discovered, that in 1800 Theodorick Crane had set in motion a revolt against the New York State government. Remember what I said earlier about Crane's life being dramatic enough without the ghost story? This is what I meant. Crane had always been a populist at heart, a belief that stemmed from his hatred of his British rulers and, perhaps even more, from his hatred of the eastern New York landlords. In his view, the Livingstons, Schuylers, and Van Rensselaers were arrogant, avaricious men who fought or served in government more for their own glory and gain than for the liberty and well being of their fellow countrymen. When he won election to the State Assembly after the war, he naturally supported such issues as election and tax reform and equitable land distribution. And he opposed the Constitution, not so much because he disagreed with its ideas but because he distrusted the men who drew it up as greedy and corrupt.

"But Crane had a serious problem that became evident in the 1790s as the first two political parties, Federalist and Republican, developed and strengthened. By temperament and philosophy he was a Republican, opposed to a powerful national government, opposed to a national debt, supportive of the needs of the yeoman farmer vis-à-vis those of the urban manufacturer, and sympathetic to the French Revolution, especially after Great Britain declared war on France in

1793. Crane was by nature a Republican, but so too were some of eastern New York's most powerful families, including the Livingstons and Clintons. Crane refused to ally himself with the leaders of New York Republicanism, and his independent spirit made him a pariah in the State Assembly and ensured that he would never climb very high on the political ladder.

"Crane's attitude towards the French Revolution is key. I'm sure you know, Tom, how popular societies formed in the years 1792 and 1793 to express their solidarity with the French revolutionary cause. They wore tricolors and liberty caps, they sang the "Marseillaise," they drank French wine and offered toasts to their sister republic. They fired salutes with cannon from the rooftops. Crane was right there with the most enthusiastic of France's supporters, founding popular societies in both Albany and Kingston.

"But the larger enemy, the Federalists, were in complete control of New York's government by 1794, and this spurred Crane into action. He accused his enemies of openly trying to arrange an alliance between the United States and Great Britain against the French and American people. He predicted, correctly as it turned out, that the Federalists would even curtail American freedoms if that's what it took to defeat France's allies in America. And in a proposal that shocked even the most anglophobic Republicans, he called for an alliance with the French to challenge and defeat the Federalists."

"Which made him quite a few enemies," I said.

"Enemies everywhere," Ben affirmed. "In 1799 he was driven out of Mohawk County by a Federalist judge on the pretext of violating the Sedition Act. He fled north to the Adirondack wilderness. Rumors circulated, proved true by Crane's own correspondence, which Hiram uncovered, that Theodorick was plotting a rebellion against the Federalists, starting in Clinton Falls and spreading from county to county until it engulfed all of New York State and eventually all of the United States. Rewards were posted and man-hunts organized, but no one could find the fugitive.

"But by late 1799 the danger had subsided," I said. "By passing the Alien and Sedition Acts and actually enforcing them the Federalists had shot themselves in both feet."

"Right," Ben said. "And it looked like Clinton Falls was about to be returned to the Republicans. So Crane returned home with the intention of resuming his role as party leader. The Federalists, desperate now, were determined to stop him. Then, in February 1800, a few days before Crane was scheduled to make his triumphant return before his fellow Republicans, John Coffey walked into Crane's house, sneaked up behind him as he sat in a bathtub, and slit his throat from ear to ear."

"Was there a trial?" I asked. I was thinking of Martha Crane's portrait of Crane carrying a Molotov cocktail and French tricolor.

"There was an inquest in 1804 when Joseph Crane returned to take over his father's farm," Ben said. "But Coffey had been dead for two years by then, so there was not an actual trial."

"Coffey was accused and found guilty?"

"Yes. Joseph Crane produced the murder weapon, a knife that belonged to Coffey. That alone was enough to convince the judge and jury, who, along with the rest of the town, probably wanted to forget about the whole affair and get on with their lives."

"Are there records of this investigation?"

"The records themselves were destroyed in a fire. The only extant source is Joseph Crane's memoirs."

"Which Langley called 'elusive, incomplete and unreliable,' " I said. I looked at Julianne. "And which the Radissons claim tells the story of Cornflower's ghost."

Ben was about to respond when Julianne, still staring into the fire, asked why they felt such a need to steal the documents.

"Let's go back to 1876 and to Hiram Crane," Ben said. "It's been said that having a scoundrel for an ancestor adds luster to the family name. Not so in the case of Hiram Crane, who believed his family name would be damaged beyond repair if his ancestor's plot was revealed in such times. You must understand this. The Civil War had ended a short eleven years before, the Centennial was at hand, westward expansion and the Indian wars were at their peak, white Americans were convinced that their nation was destined to achieve greatness. Hiram certainly believed this. He was a prosperous landlord and banker who fully expected to rise to the top of society. And like so many of his contemporaries who believed in a rising American empire, he confirmed his love of country by celebrating his roots. But the nature of his roots forced him to invent before he celebrated. So he confiscated all the documents he could find dealing with Theodorick Crane's plot, hid them in the attic, and revised his great-grandfather's biography by eliminating the undesirable aspects of it."

"What was left to steal?" I asked.

"There were other documents that Hiram Crane didn't know about and didn't discover. Remember, in his day there were no computer databases to scan or holding catalogs to consult. He could only work with what he could find, and that was a limited amount of material. Moreover, Hiram's only son, William, for reasons unexplained, had decided upon his father's death to scatter the family papers in over a dozen different archives throughout New York State. He did this in the early 1950s under a signed agreement with each institution that the papers remain closed to everyone outside the family until ten years after his death. Those dealing with Theodorick Crane's plot ended up in the State Archives in Albany, filed as miscellaneous Revolutionary War papers, where Martha found them in the winter of 1970, right before she started attending our political history seminars."

"When did William Crane die?" I asked.

"In July 1964," said Ben, "making it essential that Crane's papers be in her hands by July 1974, when they were scheduled to go public. Martha located Crane's papers in January 1970. The Weatherman incident took place in May. My guess is that sometime in that four month span Martha and Harold agreed that she would help him graft Crane onto his ancestral tree if he helped her confiscate the papers. Then they convinced us to help."

"But why?" I asked.

"We each had our reasons," Ben answered. "Martha wanted to cover up Crane's execution of Cornflower, which was a much more explosive issue in the 1970s than it had been a century before. Harold, as I've explained, wanted to use Crane's story for political purposes. It was a good recipe for success: a Vietnam War veteran connecting the ideals of a Revolutionary War hero with a call for reform and regeneration in a disillusioned and morally uncertain age. Those who yearned for certainty, especially those who remembered World War II, were a perfect audience for Harold's mixture of Great Society liberalism and old fashioned patriotism. That he truly believes in either is doubtful, but you've both seen how well the strategy has worked. And it fit perfectly into Martha's own master plan for power: help your future husband win political office and ride his coattails to your own success."

"And now Patriot Village," I said. "Another step up the ladder."

"How high can he ascend?" Ben asked Julianne.

"He's hinted at a run for governor."

"Not the Senate?"

"He knows that governors make better presidential candidates," Julianne said.

Which makes whatever secrets your family holds even more precious, I thought to myself. Then I asked Ben, "So why did you and Langley get involved?"

"I suspect Martha and Harold concluded that they couldn't proceed alone. That's the third reason why I think Harold attended the seminar, to enlist Peter and me into their scheme.

"Peter was easy to convince. He was working on an early version of his study of the American Revolution in New York State, and Theodorick Crane was one of the most important leaders of the Revolution outside the closed fraternity of eastern New York landowners. Peter was intrigued, especially when Martha told him about Crane's post war political career and murder. Crane became a martyr to Peter, a victim of an oppressive government and power-hungry politicians, an icon of democracy and independent thought that men and women in the 1970s could admire and emulate. Martha promised him that once all the documents were collected, he could use Crane's story in his dissertation."

"And you?" I asked.

"Having become so frustrated with our political failure within the movement I needed an outlet, and this little adventure promised to provide a ready one. Besides—and in this I played right into Harold and Martha's hands—I felt I owed Harold a huge favor after he'd saved Peter and me from being purged. And I agreed with Peter that Theodorick Crane's story had to be told. Our objective was the reverse of Hiram's, to emphasize Crane's radicalism and de-emphasize his murder of an Indian woman. Of course, neither Peter nor I knew that Harold and Martha's intentions were to complete Hiram's cover up.

"It turned out to be quite an adventure. Martha procured a grant, ostensibly to catalog documents on the American Revolution in New York State but actually to find all the places where William Crane had stashed his father's papers. She also cross-referenced any documents that mentioned Theodorick Crane to ensure that Hiram Crane's revised history was not contradicted. She completed her list, to the best of my knowledge, in April 1972.

"We set to work at the start of the following semester. Getting our hands on the papers and getting them out of the various archives was a surprisingly easy process; easier, in fact, than stealing a library book. We'd reconnoiter in the morning, and Peter and Harold would hide out somewhere in the building just before lunch. At lunch, when half the staff was usually out of the building anyway, Martha would hit the fire alarm. The building would empty, Peter and Harold would procure the documents, Martha would be on lookout, and I would have my car waiting for the three of them a block or two away. They had no problem exiting most buildings with the documents because in most cases security was non-existent. We had to break into a vault on two or three occasions, but even that was easy with a little practice. And since the Crane papers were still closed to the public, no one realized right away that they weren't there.

"We carried out our thefts at all the repositories in the state where Crane's papers were held. In nine months time we burglarized the New York Public Library and the New-York Historical Society, the New York State Library in Albany, the Buffalo Historical Society, the archives at Syracuse University, and over a dozen county historical societies throughout New York State.

"We came close to getting caught once in Elmira. Someone had seen Peter and Harold exiting through the back of the building and was suspicious. They ran when they saw him, and ducked around a hedgerow before the man got a good look at them. Martha didn't make it, though, and was recognized by one of her high school teachers who was leading a class trip to the county archives. He and the archive staff and the police questioned her for an hour while I waited at the rendezvous point and Harold and Peter bided their time in a coffee shop around the corner. Martha played her part perfectly, insisting that she was in Elmira looking for material on the Second Great Awakening and that she did see two suspicious looking men running away from the building, but that they were short and looked Oriental. To my knowledge the archive staff never even realized that the papers had been stolen.

"All went well otherwise, and by the beginning of May 1973 we thought we were done. Then Peter found a final batch of Crane's sealed papers right under our noses in the special collections room of SUNY Albany. There was no question we had to get them, but Martha and I were both disturbed by the idea of stealing documents from our own university. I was teaching there, after all, and Martha's parents were benefactors."

"And Langley?"

"Peter wanted them more than any of us," Ben said with some bitterness. "He'd become obsessed with Crane's story by then and had enlarged the scope of his dissertation to make Crane its focal point. We buried our reservations and went through with the operation when Peter reminded us of how Harold had saved our skins. For two days I felt a sense of foreboding, as if something was bound to go wrong as it almost had in Elmira, as if we were quickly running out of luck. We waited until after sundown on May seventh, a Monday I think. The night was dark with clouds and a new moon. It was rainy and cold. I remember seeing a few snow flakes in the air. Most of the students had wisely stayed in their dorms.

"I remained in the car while the other three went into the library. Harold and Peter told me later that they had gotten shut out of the special collections room because the door into it automatically locked when Martha activated the fire alarm. When they eventually got in, people were returning to the building and they were too late. They didn't get the documents. They ran to the back of the building, where Martha and I were waiting in my car, got in, and screamed for me to hit the gas.

"I pulled onto a road that cut across campus and drove fast. But as we passed one of the science buildings I saw a figure ahead standing in the middle of the road. Whether I didn't have time to apply the brakes or didn't hit them on purpose because I recognized him as Garrett Hollister, I do not know. Either way I barreled into him, and he crumpled to the ground. Only when Martha screamed did I take the car out of drive.

"He was under the car, which had stalled, and inside the car I could smell his flesh being burned by the hot exhaust pipe. We sat in silence for what seemed forever. Then, like an automaton, I restarted the car, backed up, and got out. I could see his crushed skull and the burn marks on his chest and knees, the look of surprise that he carried on his face like a mask.

"Martha and Harold got out of the car a few seconds after I did. They acted quickly and efficiently, taking the keys out of the ignition, opening the trunk, and lifting Hollister's body into it. Harold guided me into the back seat and got in next to me. Martha, after checking the pavement for tire marks and blood—I thanked God it was raining!—got in the driver's seat and pulled away. Peter couldn't stop weeping."

"AND THE REST OF THE STORY," I said after saying a quiet prayer to help me digest the part of it I'd heard so far, "is that you covered up the crime, and two years later the secret was revealed."

"Yes," said Ben. "We thought ourselves fortunate to be attending a university that was seemingly in a perpetual state of construction. At that time all dormitories and academic buildings had been completed, but the gymnasium on the western edge of the campus was still being built. Early the next morning, after dropping Peter off, Martha, Harold, and I took the body to the site of the new gymnasium and buried it in an area that was supposed to have been paved over and turned into a parking lot.

"Peter was disturbed by Hollister's death more than any

of us. He began to think that the whole operation had been a mistake, that we should return all the documents and turn ourselves in. What was worse, he hadn't even read all the documents yet because Harold and Martha were hoarding them and would give up only the ones that they deemed relevant to Peter's research.

"As for me, I withdrew from the whole affair and buried myself in my dissertation, which I finished the following month. I greeted a job offer from the University of Rochester with much relief, as if it were divine salvation from an unholy place and unholy people, an opportunity to begin life anew. I think I saw Peter twice more that summer, and saw nothing of either Martha or Harold. I moved to Rochester in July.

"I remained at the U of R for almost two years until Hollister's body was found in April 1975. I read over breakfast one morning on the front page of the *Rochester Democrat & Chronicle* how a couple of workers at SUNY Albany unearthed the body while digging a foundation for a locker room annex that was not part of the original building plan. It took the police a week to identify it and another three days to find a witness who had seen a tall man in a gray Chevrolet sedan hit Garrett Hollister outside the library, place the body in the trunk, and drive way. The witness was positive that the man had acted alone, that there was no one else in the car. Then they found someone else who remembered a partial license plate and they matched it to my car. I packed a bag and wrote a letter to Peter explaining that I was going into hiding and that everyone's involvement was a safe secret. I stayed in Rochester for another two days. As I left town I saw a *Democrat & Chronicle* headline that said the identity of Hollister's killer had been discovered. Next to the article was a fairly accurate police sketch of my face.

"So I wandered around for a while, then came here. Six months before I'd won the Whitbeck Prize, a little over a

year later I was leading Preserve the Islands under the assumed name of Benjamin Fries. Looking back, as I often
do, I find myself thankful that the body was discovered.
First of all it gave the Hollisters some solace to finally have
their prodigal son returned home. I remember seeing Mr.
and Mrs. Hollister on television just after I left Rochester.
They were extremely spiritual people. Every night they
prayed for their son's well being, even though the last time
they'd seen him in 1968 he had lit their American flag on
fire and had told them that he was about to depart on a
drug-induced quest to purify himself of their fascist influences.

"I blamed the murder on the revolution. I convinced myself that I'd been sucked into its vortex and spit back out
after having internalized all of its rootless energy and violence. I believed that in killing someone I had released the
energy that I had refused to release by taking part in violent
action. And when Hollister's body was unearthed I was
born anew, transformed from Albert Hartman the revolutionary to Benjamin Fries the reformer. I was given another
chance to make the world, or at least whatever small corner
of it I ended up in, a better place.

"I wrote Peter in May, and he wrote back around Christmas 1975. He had just finished his first semester teaching at
Clinton Falls. He told me that Harold had gone to New
York City to work at an uncle's think tank and to campaign,
and that Martha had taken a leave of absence from her
graduate work at SUNY Albany and had disappeared sometime in June, to where he didn't know. Their friendship had
dissolved completely, partly because Harold and Martha remained unwilling to give up the rest of the documents, despite Peter's pleadings, and partly, I suppose, because the
burden of our crime had become as heavy upon their
shoulders as it was upon mine. Peter completed his dissertation in December 1975. He cited what little information on

Theodorick Crane it contained as having come from the privately held Crane and Radisson papers."

Chapter Eight

The fact was that we were living in a bubble, talking to ourselves, reading texts drawn from . . . some . . . twilight zone—Narcissus admiring himself in a TV screen.

—Todd Gitlin, *The Sixties*, 1993

IT WAS CLEAR AFTER FIVE MINUTES OF SILENCE that Ben had told us all he knew, or all he was willing to tell. He sat there with the gray tabby cat on his lap, his eyes focused on the orange and blue flames dancing in the fireplace. I stared out at the dim lights of the buoys, blinking in the blackness of the river night, and tried to think of something to say. But nothing came, and the uncomfortable quiet that enveloped the room was broken only by the snapping of the fire and the purring of the cat. After a few minutes of this Ben asked me to tell him again about Langley.

"He was in a car accident on the thirteenth of January," I said. "The tests showed a large quantity of alcohol in his blood. And the police report said there was an empty bottle of vodka in the car. Did Langley drink when you knew him?"

"Moderately," Ben said, "but only moderately."

"I know Langley didn't drink recently because of his epilepsy. Did he have that then?"

"Not that I was aware of. So his car went off the road."

"It slid on a patch of ice, flipped over an embankment,

and landed in Westcott Creek. And that's another thing that doesn't make sense. What was he doing so far away from home on such a cold night?"

"Where did the accident take place?"

"On Route 5 just outside the city limit." I looked at Julianne, then back at Ben. "Not far from Crane's End."

"From where?" Ben asked.

"Crane's End. That's what Julianne's aunt and uncle call their house. It sits right on the river a few hundred yards from Route 5. I wonder if Langley was on his way to confront Martha again." I turned towards Julianne. "You said they had argued earlier that evening, right? Right?"

She was staring into the fireplace, as if mesmerized by the flames, a blank look on her face. I said her name again and she snapped her head towards me. "What? Yes. But like I said, I went home. I don't know what happened next."

"So Langley never read all the Crane papers after Martha and Harold first refused to share them," I said a moment later.

"He wrote in his letter that he was at a sticking point in his work and needed Crane's story to help him out of it. But he never got the papers and ended up substantially scaling back his dissertation. He blamed Martha for that."

"Scaling back?"

Ben continued. "Well, to be more precise, he returned to his topic of New York State during the Revolution. That was his original topic, as I've said before. He had modified it sometime after Martha told him about Crane's murder. He was going to write the definitive account of anti-government protest from 1770 to 1800. He made piles of notes on the subject. It was all he did; it became an obsession. But all his research was nothing more than background for the Theodorick Crane story, which he hoped would be his triumph academically as well as politically. Without the evidence he could never tell the tale in full. So he scaled back."

"The evidence is Joseph Crane's memoirs," I said. "Why did Langley say that they were of little value?"

"I don't know, Tom."

"What happened after he wrote?"

"I don't know that either," Ben said. "The only communication I ever received from Peter was that one letter, addressed to my post office box in Watertown. I wrote him three or four times after that. He didn't respond."

"He obviously gave up on the idea of an imminent revolution," I said, thinking about all the political and professional failures that Langley had gone through over the years that I knew him.

"We all did," Ben said. "An entire generation realized in a few short weeks after Kent State that revolution itself is a chimera." Then he shook his head in what I took to be regret, and stood up and quietly collected the coffee cups and plates and took them into the kitchen. When he left the room Julianne told me that she was tired and wanted to go home. I joined Ben in the kitchen and told him we were returning to Clinton Falls.

"I regret that our reunion occurred under such dour circumstances," he said while standing over the sink. "I'm sorry I was unable to help."

"But you did," I said. "I didn't even know how the dispute between Peter and Martha started. You provided that background. More than that you explained yourself. Ever since childhood I've wondered who you were, where you'd come from, why my father insisted I stay away from you. I appreciate your openness."

Ben shut off the water and dried his hands. I moved over next to him. "Ben, a professor at Clinton Falls told me that Langley believed it was Martha who turned you in."

He turned around and leaned up against the sink. "I turned myself in," he said. "It was I who called in as the witness. I told the police that there was only one person, the driver, in the car. I gave them my own license plate number.

I did it to protect my friends. They were, after all, innocent."

I stared at him, dumbfounded.

"Tom, about your father . . . " Ben stopped talking and smiled. "Like I said before, he was a good man. Get your friend home. She's had enough of the North Country."

I turned around and saw Julianne in the doorway, then turned back to Ben. "Here," I said as I took twenty dollars out of my pocket and handed it to him. "A true donation."

WE SAID OUR GOOD-BYES and were back on the road by eight o'clock. By nine-thirty Julianne was beseeching me to find somewhere to eat. We were just outside Boonville again, so I pulled into town and parked in front of the Adirondack Diner. It was closed, though, and the only illuminated building in the vicinity was the Logger Inn two doors down. We walked into it, a tavern with wood floors and walls that smelled of spilled beer and mold and boasted the best burger this side of Lake Placid. Both Julianne and I took them up on their claim. I ordered a beer for myself and a gin and tonic for Julianne.

Julianne set her drink on the table and walked over to the jukebox. While she stood there making her selections I caught myself admiring how well her blue jeans fit around her thighs and buttocks and how the dim lights of the bar shined in her hair. Then I heard the slow, quiet bass guitar of Otis Redding's "Dock of the Bay," and Julianne turned around and smiled and motioned for me to join her on the small dance floor in front of the jukebox. I drank the rest of my beer, walked over to her, and put my arms around her waist. We swayed in time to the voice of Otis Redding, a voice at once sad, desperate, and content.

"You dance slower than Fonzie," Julianne said when the song was through. She was still smiling, and had her arms draped around my neck.

"What do you expect? People have been known to jump from the dock of the bay listening to that song."

Julianne laughed softly. "It was that kind of evening wasn't it? If the river weren't frozen, maybe one of us would've jumped." Then the old jukebox lifted one forty five and replaced it with another, and she pulled away from me and started swaying her hips to the sounds of Sam Cooke's "Twistin' the Night Away." "This should provide some relief," she said.

I moved away and leaned up against the jukebox. At the bridge Julianne clapped her hands in time and bent her body backwards, still swaying from side to side. "Pure joy," she whispered, her eyes gleaming now, her smile radiant. Sam Cooke transported her, like Louis Armstrong had that night at Louie's. She'd been carried, in less than forty-eight hours, from a trough of fear and anxiety to a crest of pure joy. Her exuberance astonished me.

I wondered what she thought of Sam Cooke. In his musical world escape seemed easier than it was in ours: pop open a Coca-Cola, grab your girl, and twist your troubles away. His world also seemed simpler, without credit cards or student debt, without career or family worries, with Coke rather than beer or gin in the icebox and popcorn on the table, with nothing more than a long workweek separating party from party.

But there was an unmistakable edge in Cooke's voice that belied the joy of the party and the dance, a sorrowful edge that Julianne surely understood. Both knew that pure joy was a fleeting thing, a wonderful thing precisely because it was so rarely obtained and never dulled by familiarity.

Then I remembered Cooke's fate, dying by the bullet in a series of events that, like the events surrounding the deaths of Langley and Crane, remains full of questions. When the song ended I walked past Julianne to the table.

Julianne snapped her fingers in front of my face as I passed her. "You weren't listening," she complained after we'd sat down. I had heard her talking about something as the song ended, but I didn't know what. "I was lecturing you on the glories of soul music and the black American experience."

"Sorry," I said. "I should know better. I try to lecture three times a week to people whose minds are elsewhere."

"Where's yours?" she asked after each of us had taken a few bites of what was indeed a very good burger.

"Where's my what?"

"Your mind."

I wiped the corners of my mouth. "Still in the Thousand Islands."

"What do you think?" Julianne asked. "About Ben."

"I don't know yet. I guess I was pretty naïve to think all these years that I really knew him."

"You knew Ben Fries. It was Albert Hartman you didn't know. You said yourself they were two different people. And he was good to you. What he did over twenty years ago can't change that."

"Why did he tell us?" I said more to myself than to her.

"He trusted you," she answered. "It's not like we're a couple of newspaper reporters investigating the mystery of Garrett Hollister's death."

I looked at her and smiled. "My father owned and edited a newspaper for over twenty years."

"Oops. Insert foot into mouth."

"It's OK. I don't think he was ever too keen on investigative reporting," I said. "Are you satisfied?"

"With Ben's story?"

I nodded.

Julianne used a napkin to wipe the sweat off her neck and brow. "I don't know," she said.

"The albatross has been lifted. Crane's not really your ancestor. Aren't you relieved?"

"Sort of. But why would my parents lie to me? Why would Aunt Martha lie to me? Why would she insist that

Crane's my ancestor? There's something more to it than what we know."

"Your aunt said you were seeing psychiatrists."

Julianne's eyes narrowed. "When did she tell you that?"

"The day I visited her office. The day she threatened me."

Julianne sat back and exhaled. "I'd been receiving counseling for awhile," she said, "but I'm not currently. I'd gotten to a point where psychiatry seemed to cause more problems than it solved. I was being told to let go of my past, to discover myself within me rather than in some distant family myth. It didn't work, though. The more I separated myself from the story the more confused I became." She smiled sardonically. "I skipped about a half dozen appointments until Dr. Whatever finally got the idea." She took a sip of her gin and tonic and continued. "Remember what I said about being afraid of Cornflower's ghost?"

"Yes."

"In one of my recurring nightmares I'm being murdered by her. She's as real in my dreams as she is when I see her."

"I know about your nightmares," I said. "Your aunt told me that too."

Julianne pursed her lips.

"Your nightmare, in fact, reminded me of one of my own," I said. "It was about a scarecrow that would walk out of my closet and rip my arm off. He was short and ugly, like a troll. Not at all like the scarecrow in *The Wizard of Oz*. It got so bad that I couldn't sleep at night. I was afraid to close my eyes. Finally my mother told me to very politely ask the scarecrow to please not rip my arm off. Or, if he'd already ripped it off, to please give it back. When I had the dream again I did what my mom told me to do. The scarecrow took my arm anyway. So I asked him in my sweetest boy scout voice to please give it back. He ate it. What did I do in the dream? I went downstairs to the kitchen and got a carving knife, walked back up to my room, hacked off the scarecrow's arm, and attached it to my body. End of night-mares."

Julianne sat silent, staring at me with a slack jaw.

"There's a sequel. When my parents and brother died the scarecrow came back, made more hideous and frightening by alcohol and grief, this time dragging my parents and younger brother behind him in chains.

"When I was in Florida I had no idea whether I'd come back to school. But then, one day in November, Langley called me and reassured me that everything was OK. He got me thinking about history again. He helped bring me back from that abyss, Julianne. He gave me a worthwhile distraction from my pain and anger. He helped me beat the scarecrow."

She hesitated for a moment before quietly saying, "So what do you advise me to do?"

"Accept the fact that Theodorick Crane and Mary Strong have nothing to do with your life. Cut them off."

"I wish it were that easy. This is no scarecrow in my dream, Tom. This is an Iroquois squaw with an attitude, a genuine historical figure come back from the dead. It doesn't matter that my mother and Uncle Harold aren't descendants of Theodorick Crane. Like Ben said, my uncle grafted Crane onto his family tree. Cornflower is part of the package whether I like it or not; he grafted her on too. I can't saw off her branch like you hacked off your scarecrow's arm." Julianne hesitated and shook her head. "Besides, Tom, I've seen her. Why would she have appeared to me if she didn't want something from me? If she didn't want to harm me?"

I sat back and tried to interpret the dark look in Julianne's eyes. "What do you think Langley would have told you if you'd had a chance to talk to him?"

"I don't know."

"Do you think he would've told you that Crane wasn't really your ancestor? Maybe the same story Ben told?"

"I said I don't know."

"Why'd you come here, Julianne?"

She looked away.

"Why'd you come here?"

"To hear Ben's story. It was your idea."

"No. Why'd you come to Clinton Falls? You could've written Langley. You could've called him. Instead you drove three thousand miles just to ask him about a ghost story that you falsely believed was a family legend."

She turned away. A moment later she tugged a lock of hair and licked her lips, then turned back to face me. "My parents got divorced four years ago, and right after that my mother started seeing psychiatrists and went on medication. My father put her through hell. The bastard drove her to a nervous breakdown and then convinced her that she was the problem.

"She'd always told me stories about Theodorick Crane. At first, when I was a child, she only told the heroic ones: Theodorick and the Indian captive on Schoharie Creek, Theodorick and his small band of daring heroes fending off the Indians and saving the lives of an entire brigade of men, Theodorick at Fort Montgomery keeping up the morale of his men, Theodorick in his last years fighting the good fight against oppression and corrupt government. But around my eleventh birthday the stories slowly became more sinister. Theodorick became a murderer of an innocent Indian woman, a deserving victim of her vengeful ghost. Cornflower became the hero. I remember the tone of her stories changed when my father really began to hurt her. That's when I started hating him. And that's when the stories really started to scare me.

"A year after the divorce my mother finally gave in and killed herself. I remember seeing the look of satisfaction on my father's face when he heard the news. I remember dreaming again about Cornflower the night she died. When I left for college a week later, my father told me good-bye, gave me a car, and sent me off without trying to convince me to stay. His indifference made me hate him even more.

"Right after that I changed my name from Markbright to Radisson, in honor of my mother. I refused to let him dominate me like he dominated my mother. I didn't see him for over two years. Then, a week before last Christmas, he wrote me a long letter, an apology in the Greek sense. He invited me home for the holiday. For some reason I accepted. I arrived home on Christmas Eve. That's when I found the letter in a desk drawer. It was addressed to me and was from H. Paul Gass, the president of the First National Bank of Clinton Falls. The letter informed me that an anonymous benefactor had set up a trust fund in my name, worth over two hundred thousand dollars, to be turned over to me on my twenty first birthday.

"The next day we had Christmas dinner together. It was quite civil, actually, probably because my father had stopped drinking a month before. I asked him about the trust fund. He admitted that he'd known about it for years, and told me I could call the bank on Monday and arrange for a transfer to take place on my birthday."

"But my father wouldn't tell me who my benefactor was. I pressed him for an answer, but he refused to give one. Then, on Christmas night, I dreamed of Cornflower again. She said she knew who my benefactor was. She said there was a connection between my patron and Theodorick Crane. When I asked my father about it in the morning, he suggested I get in touch with Dr. Langley. That's all he would say."

"How did your father know about Langley?"

"I don't know. Maybe he read one of his books."

"Langley didn't publish anything, period," I said. "And I doubt your father had access to his dissertation."

Julianne said nothing.

"So why didn't you write him?"

"Cornflower challenged me, Tom. I had to take it up. I

knew from my childhood that she was here in Clinton Falls. I had to come here. The next day I packed a few bags and started to drive."

"Have you found your benefactor yet?"

"I found her my first day in Clinton Falls," Julianne said.

"Who?" I asked, already knowing the answer.

"Take a wild guess," she said, and then grabbed her coat and walked out to the car.

"Your aunt Martha," I said to the closing door. "She said she brought you to Clinton Falls to get you away from your father."

WE PULLED UP to my apartment building at twelve thirty, having encountered some snow east of Utica but not enough to slow us down. Julianne had broken our long silence as we pulled off the Thruway by asking me if she could spend another night on my couch. I agreed.

When I followed Julianne through the door the first thing I saw was the red light of my answering machine blinking like a beacon in the dark. I turned on a lamp and pressed the machine's replay button. There were two messages from Mindy, who wanted to talk, and one from Jens telling me that he had some important information and that I had to call him back when I got home, no matter what time it was.

Julianne was asleep on the couch by time I picked up the phone, her left foot dangling onto the floor, her mouth open, her breasts rising and falling softly as her breathing carried her into the private world of dreams.

I dialed Jens' number and let it ring fourteen times before hanging up. My phone rang ten seconds later.

"Hello?" I said.

"This is Jens."

"Your machine broken?"

"I turned it off."

"Why didn't you pick up?"

"I had to make sure it was you. Where have you been?"

"I'll tell you later."

"Have you seen Julianne?"

"I can see her right now. She's asleep on my couch."

"She is? On your couch?"

"Yes, Jens. Talk."

"Are you sure she's asleep?"

I snapped my fingers in front of her face. "Positive."

"OK." Jens hesitated. "I know who the mystery man is, Tom. Heinrich and I were at The 357 tonight. I saw him and his wife in one of Louie's photographs. Your uncle and Louie renovated their house."

"Who is he, Jens?" I asked, my heart racing as I remembered that Jens had seen Julianne talking with him that other night at Louie's.

"His name is Quincy Markbright. He's Julianne's father."

"Julianne's fa—"

"Quiet!"

I bit my lower lip. "Was there a date on the back of the photo?"

"November 1975. I knew he was the mystery man the moment I saw him. He looks older now, of course, but it's the same man."

"What's he doing here? What was he doing here in 1975?"

"I don't know. But Louie said that Markbright and Radisson had a much-publicized dispute about fifteen years ago over an abandoned warehouse Markbright bought on Radisson's suggestion. Markbright has lost a substantial amount of money because of the building's depreciation."

"You have to tell Julianne," I said after a long pause.

"Not quite yet."

"It's her father, Jens."

"I know, but I have my own score to settle first."

"And what are you going to do?"

"I am not sure exactly. Get the video, Tom."

"I will," I said, and hung up.

I WENT TO BED, but was unable to sleep as thoughts of Julianne Radisson and Quincy Markbright wrapped around each other like strands in a double helix. Her father! What was he doing in Clinton Falls? Why had he accused Jens of disrupting the Patriot Village unveiling? How did he know that Langley knew about Theodorick Crane and Mary Strong? Pondering these questions and their connections exhausted me, but every time I approached the edge of sleep I was jolted awake by what I thought was the faint whisper of the scarecrow, warning me that neither my parents and brother nor Langley had satisfied his appetite for death.

Then, just after four thirty, as I once again approached the edge of sleep, Julianne walked into my room and got into my bed, dressed only in a t-shirt and panties. She thanked me for relieving her of her albatross, apologized for not giving serious attention to my problems, and kissed me softly on the forehead and then full on the lips. I returned the kisses and lifted the t-shirt over her shoulders, and smiled as her hair fell back into place over the most beautiful female body I had ever seen, soft yet hard, supple yet strong, with skin glowing like alabaster in the soft moonlight that shone through my bedroom window. She kissed me again, long and deep, then reached down and massaged me with her thumb and forefinger until I was hard and a little wet. Then she kissed my chest and moved downward, her breasts brushing against my abdomen and her tongue working magic against my most sensitive skin. She slipped out of her underwear, placed me inside her, and closed her eyes and rotated her hips to some timeless and unsung melody.

Chapter Nine

One becomes moral as soon as one is unhappy.

—Marcel Proust, *Within a Budding Grove*, 1918

MY DREAM WAS FRESH AND CLEAR IN MY MIND when I heard the doorbell ring at ten Monday morning.

I was walking along a path on the south side of Washington Park, past a twelve foot high statue of Moses that overlooks Washington Lake, when I heard a disturbance on the parade ground up the hill to my left. I ascended the hill and stepped right into the middle of what seemed to be a Revolutionary War re-enactment, with Patriots and Redcoats firing into each other's ranks, and officers to the side yelling out orders. Leading the Patriots were the figures from Martha Radisson's paintings and Harold Radisson himself dressed in his lieutenant's uniform. As I stood watching the scene, a piece of shot flew past me and tore a chip of bark off a maple tree to my left. Then a British soldier fired off a round of artillery that sailed through the air and crashed into the top floor of a brick building across the street.

Frightened, I turned and ran back the way I came. But my path was blocked by a company of British soldiers on the advance. I stopped and crouched behind the statue. Peeking out, I saw more soldiers marching out of the muddy water, their uniforms incongruously clean and dry. As they moved closer I saw that the troops were neither American nor British: I could not distinguish their allegiance. Behind them, standing in a canoe, was the silhouetted figure of a long-haired woman who I presumed to be Cornflower. Then Theodorick Crane ran down the hill, bound up the statue, steadied himself against Moses' staff, and began reading Jefferson's words about self-evident truths. Cornflower saw him and began paddling forward past the emerging troops. She reached the shore, leapt out of the canoe, and directed the remaining soldiers forward. When they reached the shore behind her they raised their guns, aimed, and fired towards the statue.

The dream ended with Theodorick Crane being shot off the statue and crashing to the ground at my feet, and with Harold Radisson running towards him with an anguished look on his face and being shot to death himself as he ordered the soldiers to stop firing their guns.

I sat up in bed and used the sheet to wipe the sweat from my face and chest. My bedroom was filled with sunlight, and a large patch of it fell on Julianne's back and buttocks as she lie on top of the covers, asleep and still, her legs bent and slightly apart and her head resting on her hands. I got up, slipped into a pair of blue jeans and a t-shirt. Despite the contentment that the sunny day and the sight of Julianne should have provided I knew that the dream was a bad omen, an unstable air mass crossing over my mental and emotional landscape, pushing away whatever joy the previous night had given me and replacing it with this day's distress.

"Tom!" Mindy said when I answered the door. "I've been trying to get in touch with you since yesterday." She looked at me quizzically. "Did you just get up? Are you OK?"

"Fine, Mindy. Just tired. Can I call you later?"

"You'd better. I had a conversation with Martha Radisson this morning. She seems to think you and I are colluding against her. What have you been doing?"

"I'll call you later."

"My complaint against Walsh was denied. We're meeting this afternoon to discuss that issue among others."

At that moment, the worst possible one, Julianne walked out of the bedroom in my bathrobe, poured a glass of water from the kitchen faucet, and began opening and closing drawers. "Do you have any ibuprofen?" she asked. Then she saw Mindy. "Oh."

"Oh," Mindy parroted. She looked right at me, anger and hurt in her eyes. "You have company. Excuse me."

"We got back late from visiting a friend of Langley's in the Thousand Islands," I said. "Julianne's right, Mindy. Theodorick Crane did murder Mary Strong. Langley was involved in covering up the story. He and Martha were friends in the early seventies."

Mindy wasn't listening. She stared at me for a moment then stuffed a yellow piece of paper into my hands. "The meeting's at three at Rasheed's house. Take a look at this if you're still awake after your next fuck." She slammed the door hard as she walked out.

Julianne stood in the middle of the living room with her eyes turned down, looking ridiculously waifish in my large robe. "I'm sorry, Tom."

I walked right past her into my bedroom and closed the door hard to make it clear I didn't want her to follow.

I was shaving and reviewing in my mind the lecture I'd have to give in two hours when I unfolded the sheet of paper Mindy had given me. It was a leaflet penned by Alexa Ortiz imploring all history graduate students to attend a rally that afternoon in opposition to a new set of assistantship requirements that the committee had drawn up without consulting GOSH. The flyer was accusatory, belligerent, portentous; I felt my stomach tighten as I read it a second and third time, and was almost overcome with dread at the day's impending confrontations.

Julianne was still on the couch when I emerged from the bedroom.

"You have nice stuff," she said, presumably referring to the watercolors painted by my mother and the cabinets and roll top desk built by my father.

"I have to go," I said. "I have to teach soon. Plus I have a meeting today at two. Stay here as long as you like, though. I'll be back late this afternoon." I placed a spare key on the kitchen counter. "If you leave before I get home be sure to lock the dead bolt."

She sat up and pulled the robe over her body.

"Call me, Julianne. I still want to get a hold of Joseph Crane's memoirs." I put on my coat and walked out the door.

I HAD MISSED HALF of a beautiful day. Small, white cumulous clouds floated across an otherwise clear blue sky, and were propelled by a southern breeze that made this the first day all year that could be tolerated without scarf, gloves, and hat. It was the type of day that reminds us upstate New Yorkers that even the worst of winters can be tolerated given the certain promise of spring. I unzipped my coat and listened to the melting snow drip from the eaves of my apartment building.

Class wasn't until twelve thirty, so I walked to campus, along Perimeter Road, up the steps of the podium, and into the administration building. I bounded up the stairs two at a time, as if by hurrying to my destination I could outrun the rational warnings I issued to myself not to go there.

Martha Radisson was in the receptionist parlor hunched over the secretary's desk, pen in hand.

"I called the Chemung County Historical Society the other day looking for Theodorick Crane's papers," I said loudly as I approached. "They told me they'd been misplaced."

Martha looked at her watch, then raised her head and met my gaze. "Mr. Flanagan. I didn't expect to see you until the department meeting later this afternoon."

"I've been looking all over for his papers, in fact, but

they seem to have disappeared. I've called Buffalo, New York, Albany; no one seems to know where they are."

"You've read Crane's papers for Dr. Langley," she said calmly. "They're right here in the Center."

"Not the stolen ones. Not the ones you refused to share with him. Where are they Dr. Radisson?"

Any surprise she may have felt didn't show on her face. She straightened up and put her hands on her hips. "Come into my office."

We sat down simultaneously. I looked past her towards a massive icicle that hung from the roof and looked like an abstract sculpture framed by the office window.

"Why are you so curious about Theodorick Crane?" Martha asked, unruffled.

"Because Dr. Langley was so curious about him in the early seventies."

She smiled slightly. "If you must know, Crane was one among many Peter hoped to use as the intellectual founding fathers of a new New Left, more moderate and more in touch with the general population than SDS ever was. In all honesty, Tom, I don't think he had the vision or discipline to see the project through."

"There's another reason I'm curious. You and Dr. Langley were arguing about Crane and Cornflower on the night he died."

Martha narrowed her eyes and gave me a curious look. "How do you know to ask these questions, Mr. Flanagan?"

"Julianne interrupted your argument, don't you remember?"

"What else did she tell you?"

"That Langley was drunk that night."

"Stop playing games," Martha said, her face now the color of a ham. She picked up a pen, twirled it around in her hand, and stared at it for a moment. Then she sighed and tossed the pen onto her desk. "Peter began pressing for the Crane papers again around the first of the year. He demanded I turn them over on the night of his accident. He was drunk, like Julianne said. I told him, emphatically, that he was not going to get the documents. He made his exit and that was the last I saw of him. Three hours later he was dead. I'm as sorry as you are about all this, Mr. Flanagan."

"His car went off the road near Crane's End," I said.

"I know. He assured me before he left my office that he was going to get the papers anyway he could. I presume he was planning on taking them forcibly."

"Were you home? Did you hear anything?"

"Yes and no. I was home and I was asleep. My bedroom faces the river. There's no way I could've heard anything. I find it terrible and tragic that Peter would do something like that to himself. Do you think I'm so callous as not to be saddened by it?"

To say what I really thought would lead nowhere but into a pointless argument, so I returned to the original subject. "Why wouldn't you share the papers?" I asked. "What about Crane's life is so damn secret? Was he really plotting a rebellion?"

Martha smiled again. "Why would I tell you after refusing to tell Peter all these years?"

"Clarify something for me, then. I've heard two versions of Crane's murder: that he was killed by Cornflower's ghost and that he was killed by John Coffey, his political rival. Oddly enough both versions seem to come from the same source, Joseph Crane's memoirs. But Langley wrote in his dissertation that Joseph Crane's memoirs were 'elusive, incomplete and unreliable.' I don't understand the contradiction. I don't want to believe Julianne's ghost story, but she's so convinced that it's true that I can't help wondering—"

"Where is Julianne, Tom?"

"She's at my apartment. Probably still in my bed." When I saw Martha's face turn red again I realized I'd crossed the Rubicon. So I kept marching straight into Rome. "Which reminds me of something else. Two things actually. It was cruel of you not to tell Julianne the truth about her ancestry."

Martha's eyes widened slightly. "What?"

"Theodorick Crane's not her ancestor," I said. "The ghost story she's been so terrified of has nothing to do with her family. You could have saved her a lot of grief, Dr. Radisson. But I suppose her grief was a small price to pay for the political rewards your husband drew from the false family tree."

She looked right at me, her eyes steady and bright. "What was the second thing, Mr. Flanagan?"

"Julianne's father is in town. Quincy Markbright. I think he's been following her." I waited for a response. "And he was at the Patriot Village demonstration. He pointed the finger at Jens."

She leaned back in the chair and exhaled slowly. "Julianne's father wants to meet with her. I won't let him."

"He doesn't seem to think so. They were talking just the other night outside Louie's."

"I assure you, Tom, he won't touch her."

"Why not?"

"Because, unlike you, he understands the consequences of meddling in Julianne's affairs."

I stood up again and grabbed my coat. "Julianne also said something about a benefactor."

"You've been warned, Tom."

"Could it be that her father came to town wanting to get some of the money? Maybe he has some debts to pay off on that warehouse. Maybe, like you, he wants to keep Julianne away from the truth."

Martha turned around to face the windows. "Get out," she said quietly.

I did. But as I walked out the door I glanced back and saw her shoulders rise and fall, and saw her wipe her eye with a knuckle.

AFTER DELIVERING an uninspired yet competent lecture on the battle of Saratoga I walked to Hammond Hall and into the history department conference room, where six faculty members were involved in three different one-on-one conversations: Stanley Batcher with Roberta West, Seamus McNally with Martin Langstrom, and Roger Whittaker with Martha Radisson, who was still fuming with anger. All six held two-year renewable terms except Stanley Batcher, Langley's replacement on the committee. He had been on the committee since it became the department's power broker five years before, when the university faced the threat of deep budget cuts at the hands of the state Board of Regents.

What struck me most about the budget crisis, more even than the committee's power grab, was the acrimony it had caused between the university faculty and the citizens of Clinton Falls. It all began when the president revealed his proposed cuts, which called for the dismissal of faculty and staff along the proportions of two-to-one. A professor from the Political Science Department wrote a letter to the *Clarion* saying that if any group at the university was indispensable, it was the faculty. Staff positions should be eliminated, he argued, and students should be given the responsibility of cleaning up after themselves and maintaining the university infrastructure.

Readers of the *Clarion* were appalled. Letter after letter arrived, hundreds of them, saying the same thing: if anyone was dispensable it was the arrogant professor who worked for ten hours a week, fifteen if he or she taught a graduate course, and lived off what one writer called state sponsored academic welfare. One correspondent went so far as to read and critique the Political Science professor's award winning book. She complained that after spending fifty dollars buying it and three whole days reading its two hundred pages, she was none the wiser. Even *The Chronicle of Higher Education* picked up on the dispute. That article was written by a

sociologist at Yale who had never been to Clinton Falls and
used the controversy as an example of how "serious aca-
demical pursuits and small town bowling alley mentalities
simply do not mix."

In the end the budget crisis passed—three quarters of a
million dollars were cut from the university's budget instead
of the threatened four million—but as the angry voices of
complaint quieted, town and gown never resumed their re-
luctant tolerance of one another.

I sat down between Professors West and Langstrom as
Whittaker greeted me with a stern, scolding look.

"Flanagan. We were just talking about you," he said.

"Considering me for the full time position, I hope." I
looked at the dour faces around the table and saw that the
topic of discussion, whatever it was, left no room for humor.

Whittaker held up Alexa's flyer. "There's been some concern about this."

"I didn't know a thing about it until this morning," I said.

Martha Radisson locked onto my eyes. "First the Patriot
Village protest, now this? You're supposed to work with us,
Mr. Flanagan, not against us, especially now that you're in
the classroom. How are we supposed to accommodate
graduate student interests when you subvert our good faith
attempts by making us look like tyrants?"

"Ask Alexa," I said.

"We're asking you," Whittaker snarled.

Seamus McNally held up a palm. "Take it easy, Roger."

Whittaker ignored him. "The bylaws stipulate that graduate students are allowed a representative on this committee
at the discretion of the faculty. Your group is making things
difficult for us with its public subversion."

"I want to arrive at an accommodation just as much as
you do," I said, "probably more. I'm telling you, it's Alexa
Ortiz and her group that's making the situation difficult."

Martha Radisson moved forward in her chair. "What are

you going to do, Tom, go on strike? Is that what this afternoon's rally is all about?"

"If it were up to me I'd try communicating," I said.

She was furious now. "Communicate! When you're ready
to communicate with words instead of fists, come see us.
For now, any action you take against this committee will im-
peril your academic well-being."

"There's no reason to make this personal," said Seamus
McNally, a large man with a bald head and hairy arms. He
was the senior faculty member in the department and one
of the most respected academics in the entire SUNY system. "Look, Tom, the fiscal crisis is only dormant. If the
university administration gets wind of the true nature of our
internecine warfare, we'll be easy prey when the next budget
axe falls."

"And until you agree to join our united front," Dr. Radisson said vehemently, "I move that we dismiss you from this
committee."

"Motion seconded," said Dr. Batcher.

"So be it," said Whittaker, scribbling something in a
notebook.

"Let's at least take a vote, Roger." McNally said.

Whittaker glared at him and shuffled a few papers. "All
in favor of suspending . . . " He hadn't even finished his
sentence when five hands shot up as if controlled by a solitary puppeteer.

"Your vote, Seamus?"

"Nay," he said with a slight wink my way.

AN HOUR LATER I drove to Trumbull Street, Clinton Falls'
eight block answer to Greenwich Village, and parked in a
space just vacated by a dairy delivery truck.

I was as familiar with the neighborhood as I was with any
in Clinton Falls, having lived in the upstairs flat at 271
Trumbull during my junior and senior years. The party at-
mosphere there was constant, with bars open from 8 a.m. to

4 a.m. and music floating through the night and early morning air. The local diner, Trumbull's Palate, served breakfast
food and burgers around the clock. On more than one occasion I had sat with friends in a booth at the Palate, drinking coffee by the gallon, singing "Maggie May" or "The
Night They Drove Old Dixie Down" and waiting for the
Trumbull Tavern or Smitty's or Daquari Dan's to reopen.

But I remembered other things about Trumbull Street:
the double or triple door locks used as security against the
omnipresent burglars, the cocaine and marijuana dealers
lurking in the dark, mossy passageways between buildings,
the single mothers with their wailing and undernourished
children using up their monthly food stamp allotment to
buy Doritos and Jolt cola at Franco's market, the homeless
men with the sour odor of alcohol and two or three days
grime about them taking deep swigs from quart bottles of
Boone's Farm or Old English 800 and asking passersby for
loose change. Trumbull Street was all of this, for some the
best and for others the worst that Clinton Falls had to offer.
I was glad to be living elsewhere.

Rasheed L'Overture lived in a basement flat below the
Daily Grind Café, across the street and two blocks south
from where I used to live. The windows of his apartment
were covered with curtains made from tiny fish-shaped
beads, and around the door was a set of Christmas lights
that Rasheed kept blinking all year long. He answered my
knock with a wide smile and a friendly handshake. Soukous
music blared from inside.

"Tom," Rasheed said. "You missed my Kwanzaa party."
He laughed and shook his index finger. "We were all hoping
you'd match your performance from the year before."

Rasheed Jones, from Trinidad, was six foot six and solid
as a bull. He had changed his surname some years back as a
tribute to his hero, the Haitian revolutionary Toussaint
L'Overture. I liked him because he threw a good party and
always invited whites to it and because he engaged in

classroom arguments with a rare courtesy and civility. I didn't see him around much, though, because we didn't take many of the same courses and because he spent most of his free time tutoring at-risk black students.

"I was in Florida visiting my uncle, Rash. I'm sure I missed a good one."

I looked into his apartment and saw Alexa Ortiz jump up off the couch. "Our rep is here, everybody. Now we can get down to business. Turn the music down, Rash."

Rasheed motioned me through the door and shut off the stereo. As I crossed the room I took measure of the seven other students that comprised the GOSH inner circle. Seated in a blue and green striped recliner was Marvin Ganderbast, a tall, fat, baby-faced student of Russian history who, when drunk, would deliver a side-splitting impersonation of Nikita Khrushchev. On the floor to his left was Mary Hargrove, who always dressed in shapeless black clothes and boasted the department's highest grade point average. Next to her sat her lover, Reggie Daniels, a returning student in her mid-thirties who dressed in pastels and oversize black army boots and whose incessant talking made up for her girlfriend's silence. On the couch sat Mindy and Jens, the space between them just vacated by Alexa. Sam Danvers, from Houston, sat in a folding chair on the other side of the couch and was telling Jens about the true meaning of the 1836 Texas Revolution. Next to him was Ray Dale, a small, nervous man who wore a tinted pince-nez, was working on his fifth degree at the university, and had never held a job off campus.

As I made my way across the room I ran through my mind possible scenarios and wondered who I could rely on if it came down to a decision between Alexa and her confrontational tactics and me and my conciliatory ones. Marvin Ganderbast and Sam Danvers would support me, as would Rasheed if he and Alexa were off again. But Jens, Mary Hargrove, and Reggie Daniels were in Alexa's corner, and Ray Dale, with his propensity for seeing conspiracies everywhere he looked, would probably side with her too. That left Mindy, who was already indignant at the department faculty for its refusal to support her against Walsh. She didn't even acknowledge me as I sat down next to her, and when I glanced at the side of her face I could see lingering traces of hurt and disappointment in the shadows of her eyes.

"So how'd the meeting go?" Alexa asked disingenuously.

"I got kicked out of the meeting," I said. "And was made a fool of. The committee threatened to eliminate the position of grad student rep. Can your timing be a little better next time? Or is this just what you wanted?"

"They can't just eliminate the position," Reggie Daniels said. "And if they do we should walk right in there and take them hostage until they meet our demands. Go Bucci on 'em."

"They created the position, Reggie, they can eliminate it," I said. "And let's lay off the hardball for a while."

"We're sick and tired of their domination, Tom," Reggie said.

"McNally is willing to hear us out," I said. "I'm sure he can convince others to listen."

"And Dr. Radisson?" Alexa asked, now interested.

"You can forget about her," I said.

"Why?"

"It's a long story, Alexa. Let's just say that she's probably using you to divide and conquer."

"I knew it," said Ray Dale vehemently. "Just like she was doing with Langley."

"Langley was a tight-assed, conservative bastard," Reggie Daniels said.

"Actually," said Jens, "Langley was a revolutionary. Just the wrong kind of revolutionary, pressing for the wrong kind of revolution."

"Their dispute is irrelevant now," Alexa said. "We have to take a stand."

I was looking at Jens, thinking about what he said, but didn't want to let Alexa's position go unchallenged. "What we have to do is sit down and communicate. Hammer things out issue by issue. McNally and others will listen to us, Alexa. I know they will."

"We should beat them into submission," said Reggie Daniels.

Marvin Ganderbast reached across Mary Hargrove and put a hand on Reggie's shoulder, which she shrugged off. "Shut up, Reggie," Marvin said.

"Issue by issue," I said, "starting with Dr. Walsh's grade policy and moving on to the new TA requirements and so on. We have to keep it civilized. No rallies, no strikes, no belligerent flyers."

Alexa suddenly stood up. "Our rally! We're supposed to meet the anthropology TAs in front of Hammond Hall in an hour." She looked at me. "Are you coming?"

"No, Alexa. I don't believe in those tactics."

"Marvin?"

"I'm with Tom."

"Reggie?"

"Crush them."

"Mary?"

She stood up and put a piece of chewing gum in her mouth.

"Sam?"

"I've got to work. If I miss another day, I'm as good as fired."

"Rash?"

He moved over to Alexa and put his arms around her. "I go where you go, baby."

"Mindy?"

"I agree with Tom on this one, Alexa. We have to ease up a bit."

Alexa shot Mindy a vicious glance, then turned towards Jens, smiling. "I know you're in, Jens."

He joined them standing in the middle of the room.

"Ray?"

He moved his eyes cautiously from me to Alexa. "I'll drive myself."

"I DON'T UNDERSTAND YOU," Mindy said later that afternoon on the phone. "You don't want a confrontation between faculty and students, and yet you do everything possible to incite Dr. Radisson's anger."

"My problem with Martha Radisson has nothing to do with department politics, Mindy. If she wants to bring it into that arena, it's her problem."

"And yours and mine and every other student's. She's a powerful woman, Tom."

"I know that. And she makes trouble like Betty Crocker bakes cookies." It felt good to hear Mindy laugh. "Do you remember Toby Reynolds?" I asked.

"He was Langley's TA, what, five years ago? Before we came around. I've heard stories about him."

"Do you know what Toby's doing now?"

"No."

"He's substitute teaching outside Buffalo. After eight years of graduate school, after earning a Ph. D. from Johns Hopkins, he couldn't find a job anywhere."

"The market's bad, Tom."

"This doesn't have anything to do with the market. Four years ago Martha Radisson caught him sneaking around STARCH looking for documents on Theodorick Crane and Mary Strong. She didn't say a thing about it until last year when she informed practically every history department in the country that Toby was not a viable candidate for a position because he had plagiarized material in his master's thesis. Just last year, Mindy, that's the cruelty of it. She waited until Toby completed all his work before making sure he had no future in academia."

"Who told you this?"

"Ray Dale did after our joke of a meeting."

"Ray knew about this?"

"He and Toby go way back."

"Does Ray Dale know about Theodorick Crane and Cornflower?"

"Only what I told him, which was very little. But he knows that Toby worked for Langley and hated Martha Radisson. He thinks it was part of Martha's conspiracy to take over the department."

"Are you in danger?"

"I wouldn't be surprised if Martha tries to get me suspended. But physical danger? No, not yet." I hesitated. "There are some new developments in the Theodorick Crane situation. I mentioned a couple of them this morning."

"Tell me," she said.

"How about we talk over dinner? My treat."

"Your treat?" she asked. "You're on."

WE WENT TO MAZELLI'S, the most upscale restaurant in Clinton Falls and one of the finest Italian eateries in upstate New York. I dressed well for the occasion in a pair of black slacks, maroon mock turtleneck and black silk jacket. Mindy did me one better by wearing a long sleeved dark blue dress with a string of pearls that looked real. She was waiting inside the door of her apartment building when I picked her up at seven thirty.

"I even washed my car," I said as I opened the door for her. "I didn't want us to get road salt on our expensive clothes."

Mindy laughed and got in.

Our reservation was for eight o' clock, and we arrived just as the waitress was pouring our water. My shrimp primavera and Mindy's chicken Milanese were both excel-

lent, as was the tiramasu we split for dessert. The conversation over dinner and dessert was made trivial and fun by the
bottle of Chianti we shared and was a welcome departure
from the weighty matters that Mindy and I usually discussed
as of late. I felt good for a change, about myself, about
Mindy, about the world. The morning's dark clouds seemed
an illusion now that I was safely seated at a corner table in a
posh dining room with Mindy; I was a fool to believe that
they were no longer there.

When we finished the tiramisu and coffee I paid the bill
and we went to the bar to listen to Wanda Goodwin's piano
jazz. Mindy's expression as she sat down told me that the
trivial talk was over.

"Tell me about these new developments," she said.

It took me a while because I had a lot to cover: Saturday
night with Walsh and Julianne, Sunday with Ben Fries,
Jens's phone call, my conversation with Martha earlier that
day. Mindy listened with a mixture of surprise, concern, and
sympathy.

"It goes a lot deeper than you thought, then," she said.

"And the deeper it goes the murkier it gets."

"What do you know for sure?"

"Hiram Crane and his son William covered up the family
history. Harold Radisson, Martha Crane, Peter Langley, and
Albert Hartman stole most, maybe all, of the documents
that were intended to go public. Harold Radisson grafted
Theodorick Crane onto his own ancestry. Langley was
denied access to many of the stolen papers, possibly including Joseph Crane's memoirs. And he and Martha were arguing about this whole thing on the night of his accident."

"And about Theodorick Crane and Cornflower?"

"Crane executed Cornflower, also known as Mary
Strong, in 1781. Crane himself was murdered in 1800 while
plotting a quixotic revolution against the Federalists."

"And the questions," Mindy said pointedly.

"Dozens of them, darkening the waters. What did

Langley know about Theodorick Crane? What knowledge did Martha and Harold want to keep hidden from him? What's the true nature and significance of Joseph Crane's memoirs? On and on they go."

Mindy thought it all over for a few moments, then finished her glass of wine and signaled the bartender for another.

"Why would John Coffey kill Crane?" she asked. "I mean, Crane was a pariah among the Republicans. Wouldn't the Federalists rather let him shoot himself and, by extension, his fellow Republicans, in the foot?"

"Good questions," I said. "My guess is that Langley asked the same ones."

"Which is why he said Joseph Crane's memoirs contained discrepancies."

"Exactly," I said.

The bartender brought Mindy's wine. "What are you going to do?" she asked.

"Take an even closer look at Langley's dissertation. Whittaker has his notes locked up. I'll try to get access to them to see if I can find Joseph Crane's memoirs. The frustrating thing is that traditional methods of historical investigation have gotten me nowhere. I've been through the STARCH and library holdings half a dozen times, and I've read through Langley's dissertation twice in the past week. Except for that tidbit about the memoirs, there's nothing there at all."

"All the relevant documents are out of circulation," Mindy said.

"So it seems."

Mindy took a sip of wine. "Do you believe what Julianne tells you?"

"Some of it," I said cautiously. "But I also think she's holding something back. Not lying outright, but not letting me in on everything either."

"You believe her story about Cornflower's ghost?"

"She swears by it." I sat back and exhaled. "I don't know. Maybe feeling pity for her did blind me."

The lights in the bar had dimmed, and Wanda Goodwin was playing "How Deep Is The Ocean (How High Is The Sky)." Mindy took her wine glass between two fingers and rolled it for a long moment.

"It's partly my fault," she said quietly.

"What is?"

"You being mixed up with Julianne's problems."

"What are you talking about? Getting involved with her was my decision. My responsibility."

"I saw trouble in your eyes when we talked at Louie's that night, Tom, and again that morning in the student union. I saw it even more clearly this morning. I should have been there for you, on your terms. I wasn't."

I took hold of Mindy's hand. "We split up because I was weighed down with some heavy emotional baggage, Mindy. It wasn't fair then and still isn't fair for me to expect you to be my bellhop. You're being justifiably cautious now because you're not sure whether I've unpacked or not. How could I hold that against you? Your being here tonight is more than I can ask for."

She gave a slight nod and wiped her eye with the back of her hand. When she returned her gaze to me I saw the same forgiveness in her eyes that I felt in my heart.

"Are you happy?"

The question surprised me. I took a sip of wine, then answered. "No, I'm not. I've always thought of happiness as overrated. Doing the right thing is what I usually aim for."

"Happiness and moral action are not mutually exclusive," she said. "You as a Christian should know that."

"I'm the type of person who needs someone to tell me I'm doing the right thing. Without that affirmation I don't feel the happiness."

"Someone like your father?"

"Yes, someone like my father. Since my parents died I

haven't found anyone to take his place in the affirmation department."

"Did you hope that Langley would fill that role?"

I nodded. Mindy smiled and then asked me another surprising question. "Do you remember the day we met?"

I too smiled at the memory. "Of course. It was cold and snowy. You walked into Langley's classroom without a coat or hat. Langley couldn't believe it."

"And I was wearing shoes that couldn't grip the ice. After class you gave me your coat and walked with me to make sure I didn't slip. That was the most *right* thing anyone's ever done for me here."

I took Mindy's hand again and cupped it between mine, feeling at once elated and desperate, my ears filled with Wanda Goodwin's melancholy version of "You Don't Know Me."

Chapter Ten

That blind and imbecile attachment to the most visible of all colors was to have cruel consequences.

—Adolphe Messimy, *Mes Souvenirs*, 1937

AFTER CLASS ON WEDNESDAY JENS AND I DESCENDED into the subterranean world of the Audio-Visual Department. The air grew thick and heavy and stale as we walked down the long ramp that led us to the passageways below. The smoke from Jens's cigarette mixed with the smell of formaldehyde that leaked from the biology labs on this side of the tunnels. On a dingy yellow wall outside a lab door someone had hung a long poster of a beach at sunset. Farther down, just under a caged light fixture, was a solitary graffito: "Save yourself! Turn back!"

We entered the AV production office: a large, glass walled room that could have doubled as a museum of audio visual technology from 1970 to the present. Old televisions and gray filmstrip machines were stacked in one corner against the glass wall; huge spotlights and refrigerator-sized loudspeakers filled the space to their left.

We found the man we were looking for, Gus Malinowski, in a small room off the main one sitting in front of a video monitor. The chair he was in could barely contain his bulk, and the video machine he used was like a child's toy in his long, thick fingers. He waved us in when he saw us.

"Tom Flanagan. Haven't seen you in almost a year."

"Sorry I haven't visited, Gus. I've been away."

After making introductions I glanced at the monitor and saw the dean of Undergraduate Studies explaining with the aid of bar and pie charts how the State University at Clinton Falls was attracting better students each year.

"How come they didn't sign up for my course?" I joked.

Gus looked up and smiled. "Each year the president budgets fifty thousand dollars to make a video that he sends to high school guidance counselors. My daughter saw last year's video at Clinton High and was proud as a peacock that her daddy had directed it. She still saw it for what it was." He turned his eyes back to the screen. "She's at Ithaca College now."

"Fifty thousand dollars would pay for ten adjunct positions," I said. I shook my head. "You have the tape?"

"Right here." He held up a VHS cassette. "It took some sweet talk to get it, though. My friends at WCFT can get into a lot of trouble if their footage finds its way into the wrong hands."

I looked at Jens and said, "No problem, Gus."

Gus slid the tape into the VCR as Jens and I each pulled up a chair and sat down. Gus pressed a couple of buttons, and the image of city hall appeared, noisy and crowded with people. I saw the Congressman standing in front of his well-dressed friends. I saw the audience full of dignitaries and citizens. As the image shifted I saw the Clinton Falls Crusaders walking in a circle and chanting and a policeman to the left of the protesters speaking into his radio. The image shifted again and the Crusaders became the focus of the camera's attention. There was Jens in his red shirt. There was me turning away from the camera, hiding my face.

"Stop!" said Jens.

Gus quickly pressed the pause button. I didn't need Jens' outstretched finger to direct my eyes to the distinct image of

Quincy Markbright, hands in his coat pockets, turning towards the camera.

"Can you advance it frame by frame?" I asked.

"This is a two thousand dollar machine," said Gus. "It
can do just about anything."

Gus pressed a button and Quincy Markbright moved forward in super slow motion. Then the camera moved backwards and expanded our field of vision, and Markbright's
figure grew smaller. Jens and his identifying red shirt came
back into the picture. Was it Jens that Markbright was turning towards? I waited impatiently to see what happened
next, but a few frames later Jens moved forward and
blocked Markbright from view. Then the screen went blank.

Gus hit the pause button again and sat back in his chair.
"See what you wanted to see?"

"The man in the hat accused me of disrupting the unveiling," Jens said. "But I still don't understand why."

"Maybe it was the shirt," Gus said.

"What?"

"Your shirt. One of the few things I remember from college history was a comment some French general made after
WWI about red being the most visible of all colors. That's
why German snipers had such an easy time picking them
off."

I smiled. "I've always wanted to ask you about that," I
said to Jens. "Is wearing red some kind of political statement?"

"It was my favorite color *before* I became a socialist," he
said.

Gus shook his head. "There's more to the tape, you
know," he said.

I looked at Jens. "Let's see it."

Gus hit play and the videotape resumed at full speed.
The camera was now to the left of the podium pointed up
at Harold Radisson. Then the camera moved around the
front of the podium and focused in on the dignitaries seated

behind the Congressman: Clinton Falls' mayor, the university president, a few members of the chamber of commerce. The screen went blank again, this time for only a second, and the image returned with the camera to the right of the stage, aimed at the audience. There was Louie Fratello, and there, two rows in front of him, was Martha Radisson. Then I saw it, beneath Martha's hat, a cloth or wrapping: a bandage. I reached over Gus's shoulder and pressed the pause button.

"Gus, can you zoom in on the image of Dr. Radisson?"

"We need a computer for that," he said. "Come in here."

He ejected the tape and sprung from the chair with a surprising quickness for someone his size. He led us into another room that contained two monitors and video machines hooked up to a computer. He inserted the tape, pressed a few keys on the keyboard, and said, "This image?"

"Yes, that one."

Gus moved the mouse and clicked, moved the mouse and clicked again. Each time he did so the image of Martha Radisson grew larger and fuzzier until the upper half of her body filled the screen. He stopped when the image grew too blurred to discern, then pressed a few keys. Then the image reappeared in higher definition, and I saw through her makeup and the shadow of her hat what I hadn't notice before: lacerations and bruises on the left side of her face.

"She doesn't look good," Gus said with a frown.

"How did she disguise this?" asked Jens.

"She obviously did a good job with her makeup," Gus answered.

"Then why are we noticing it now?"

"One reason is because cameras like the one used here often render the top layer of skin or makeup nearly invisible. Remember Nixon in the 1960 debate against Kennedy? He looked dirty and unshaven, but not because he hadn't shaved. This is the same effect, and it's exaggerated under magnification and high definition. Look at the difference."

Gus pressed a few keys and the image returned to its original size, with Martha Radisson looking more or less normal. Then he gave the undo command, and Martha's injuries were visible again.

But what struck me more than her injuries was the expression on her face, a combination of disorientation and subliminal fear that I had seen only on a couple of occasions and only on the faces of those who had been seriously hurt and then drugged up to relieve their pain.

"She's not supposed to be in this condition for at least another five minutes," I said.

"Where'd she get those injuries?" Gus asked. 'Was she in a fight?"

"She was in an automobile accident," I said with a glance towards Jens, "and she didn't want people to know about it. Roll it, Gus."

A few minutes later, with Harold Radisson well into his harangue, there were two successive crashes followed by a scream followed by the sight of the Congressman jumping off the rostrum to help his fallen wife. Smoke clouded the image, but I could tell that the incendiary—thrown, I now suspected, by Quincy Markbright—had landed on the other side of the model. I could tell too that Martha Radisson was the only person in the room to suffer anything worse than a minor case of smoke inhalation. But the smoke and the confusion it brought served the purpose of diverting everyone's attention from Harold Radisson, who flung his wife's hat aside, gently unwrapped the bandage from around her head, and stuffed it in his coat pocket.

Before Jens and I left Gus I gave him fifty dollars for a professional copy of the tape, and for his silence.

I TRIED ALL AFTERNOON to reach Martha Radisson, but each time I called or stopped by her office I was told by her secretary that she was either out of the building or in a meeting. So on my final visit I wrote a short note telling Martha that I had seen the videotape and knew she had been injured sometime before the unveiling, probably while in the car with Langley. I placed the note in an envelope, sealed it, and signed my name across the seal. Then I slid the envelope under Martha's office door, which I knew only she could open.

THAT NIGHT I WENT to Ash Wednesday mass. After the service I said prayers for my parents and brother, which I did every time I entered a church, and then, as an afterthought, said a quick "Our Father" for Langley.

I returned home, had a cheese and tomato omelet for dinner, and changed into a pair of blue jeans and a black turtleneck. Then I drove to Crane's End, my car sliding and fishtailing in the few inches of wet snow that had fallen late that afternoon and evening.

As I'd hoped, Julianne was the only one home. "We need to talk," I said. "Get your coat."

"We went through this the other night at Louie's," she said.

"I have something to tell you. It's important."

"Another history lesson?"

"Current events."

"Give me a minute. I need to make a phone call." she said. "And you might want to clean that grease off your forehead."

I went back to the car, and looked nervously in the rearview mirror as I waited.

We were on Monroe Avenue when she finally asked me where we were going.

"The university," I said.

I parked in the Indian Quad lot without thinking twice about the two cars that pulled in behind us and parked in the shadows a few hundred feet away. We walked down a slushy footpath to Indian Tower. Then I took out my key ring and found the master key that I still had from my years working for the AV department. I unlocked and opened the heavy glass and steel door and motioned for Julianne to walk through.

"Where are you taking me?" she said.

"To the penthouse. It's quite a view from up there."

The penthouse of each tower was nothing more than a glorified attic on the twentieth floor with white concrete walls and dingy, brown carpeting on the floor. For years the four penthouses had served as clandestine party rooms for residents of the towers. But the administration had closed them to the public a few years ago when a party on Colonial Quad got out of hand and a drunk and stoned sophomore jumped out the window and fell twenty stories to his death.

We took the elevator to the nineteenth floor, where we had to climb a flight of stairs to the twentieth. When we got there I unlocked the door to the penthouse. We entered the room and saw through the windows one of the only views on campus that rivaled the one from Martha Radisson's office. It looked south towards the snow-covered track and football field and towards the gymnasium, decorated for basketball season with rows of yellow and blue banners.

I walked to the window and sat down on the cold radiator. I told Julianne about the latest conversation I'd had with her aunt.

But she interrupted me after less than a minute. "I told her about our trip," she said.

"You what?"

"I had to find out if what Ben Fries said is true. Aunt Martha explained everything. She told me what happened to Theodorick Crane. She explained Cornflower's ghost. I'm afraid I have to agree with her, Tom. Our skeletons must remain in their closet."

"Julianne . . . "

She set her jaw and looked away. "Aunt Martha and I both recommend that you stop probing into our affairs."

"Stop probing? You came to me, if you'll recall. I never asked to hear about your family's past."

"And maybe you should just accept the fact that Dr. Langley got drunk and smashed his car." She hesitated. "I like you, Tom. I don't want to see you get hurt."

"What?"

"Forget about Langley. Leave him be. Please stop trying to resurrect him."

I moved right up to her, turned her face towards mine, and locked onto her green eyes. "What aren't you telling me, Julianne?"

She stepped back towards the wall and leaned up against it, silent. Then she walked quickly over to the door and out into the landing.

"Listen, Julianne," I said, just a step behind her, "This morning I saw a videotape of the Patriot Village demonstration. It showed that your aunt was injured before the protest turned violent, before it even began. I can't prove it, but I think she was in the car with Langley. I think that's how she got her injuries. Did she tell you about that in your conversation? And I'm pretty sure I know who threw the bomb, Julianne. It was your father."

Without answering she collapsed against the closet that housed the elevator motor, facing the stairway to the nineteenth floor. I crouched down in front of her. Her eyes were heavy and wet and full of anxiety, the energy draining from them like water from an unstopped bathtub. I assumed she was reacting to the second piece of news.

"Did you know he was in town?" I asked, speaking loudly over the whirring and grinding of the elevator motor.

Then her gaze shifted to a point in space above me and to my left, and her mouth opened in astonishment. I turned around to see what she was looking at, but was stopped by an object hitting the left side of my neck and face. My vision blurred for a second then went black. As I steadied myself against the railing I heard Julianne yell something, but I couldn't make out what it was. Another hit from behind and my head, neck, and back exploded with pain. Then I felt my arm, my hand, and the rest of my body go limp.

I CAME TO half aware, things looking hazy as if I were in the midst of a brief awakening during a restless night's sleep. After a few seconds of slowly opening and closing my eyes I saw that I was in the back seat of a car with maroon upholstery and silver trim. The head in front of me was large, and on it sat a fedora whose color I couldn't make out, but guessed was tan.

Julianne was next to him. She abruptly turned around and gasped when she saw me. Then she looked at her father with blazing eyes that seemed to illuminate the right side of his face.

I touched my forehead to see if it was bleeding, and was relieved to see only ashes on my fingertips. I moved my jaw to make sure my mouth worked and after a few attempts at speaking was able to say something intelligible. "You set me up, Julianne. That phone call you made . . . "

"It wasn't to him," she interrupted angrily. She looked at Markbright again, and again her eyes burned. "The call was to Aunt Martha. She made me promise to notify her when I saw you again. I'm sorry, Tom. I thought she wanted to talk. I had no idea it would lead to this."

"And Ben? If he gets hurt I'll never forgive you."

Julianne said nothing.

I slowly sat up. Julianne reached back to help, but I shook her off with a scornful twist of my shoulders. I caught her father's eyes in the rearview mirror.

"What's this all about?" I said.

"You shouldn't have gotten involved, Flanagan."

"I know you threw the bomb at the Patriot Village demonstration," I said in an angry rush of words. "And I know why. You can tell Harold and Martha that strong arm tactics are no more effective than bribery or blackmail. You can tell them I'm going to find out what happened to Langley and what happened to Theodorick Crane."

"Tell me where Langley's notes are and I'll spare you more grief."

"I don't know where they are."

"At your apartment? At the university?"

"I don't know."

"They're somewhere. Langley took notes on everything. As if the petty melodrama of his life actually mattered." He slammed a fist against the steering wheel. "I never should have told him."

"Told him what?" I said. "Did you tell him about Theodorick Crane?"

"Shut up, Flanagan."

We were at a stoplight. Julianne sobbed as Markbright turned around and hit me in the head, this time with the butt end of a gun.

Chapter Eleven

In the republic of scholarship, every citizen has a constitutional right to get himself as thoroughly lost as possible.

—David Hackett Fischer, *Historian's Fallacies*, 1970

I CAME TO AGAIN IN THE DAYLIGHT, not knowing what day or time it was, feeling as if all four of my wisdom teeth had been pulled without the benefit of pain killers. Startled at the sight and sound of heavy rain hammering against the window to my left, I quickly sat up and groaned at the ache in my head. I looked at my watch and saw it was eight thirty in the morning; I pressed a button and saw it was Thursday. I turned to my right and saw Louie sitting in a chair next to the window drinking coffee and reading the morning paper. It took me a moment to realize I was in a spare bedroom above The 357.

Louie stood up. "You look better, Tommy, but still pretty bad." He studied me for a minute as if to confirm his assessment and saw me staring out the window. "This weather's crazy, isn't it? Two days ago we were in an Arctic freeze. Right now it's forty and getting warmer by the minute." He sat on the edge of the bed. "You were talking in your sleep, Tommy. Markbright did this?"

"At first I thought it was Stevie Fagioli."

Louie laughed. "The Stitch would've duck-taped a hundred pounds of barbells around your chest and tossed you in the canal. Despite the fact that it's frozen solid."

I smiled at that. "How'd I get here?"

"Markbright dumped you off in the alley out back."

I touched my head. "You didn't take me to a hospital?"

"How would you pay for it, Tommy? You look like hell, but you're fine." Louie set the newspaper down and looked right at me, his face solemn now. "I stopped by your apartment last night. The door was unlocked. The place was in shambles."

I pressed against the outside of my pants pockets and felt my keys. Then I remembered the spare. "That bitch," I said.

"Julianne?"

"She stayed over the other night. I gave her a spare key."

Louie handed me a tray of coffee, orange juice, cereal, and milk. "You have to talk to the police," he said.

"No I don't."

"You don't have a choice, Tommy. Jens Erlenmeyer and three other Crusaders were arrested this morning for conspiracy to kidnap Julianne Radisson."

"What?" I grabbed the paper and saw on page one that Louie wasn't kidding.

"Detective Delaney wants to see you right away."

"Detective Delaney? Come on, Louie, he's probably in Harold Radisson's pocket just like the rest of this damn city. He'll probably botch the investigation."

"You don't have to mistrust every police officer in the nation because of one failed investigation, Tommy. The guy got away. He fled the scene of the crime."

"And the police never found him," I said.

"Neither did the Coast Guard or RCMP. Let it go, for Christ's sake. Besides, Delaney's a friend, a good man." Louie moved to the window. "And what would your father think of you trying to bring down the Radisson family? Do you think he'd approve? Will you ever let up?"

"I'll let up when I find out the truth about Langley.

Louie, did you notice anything strange about Martha Radisson at the Patriot Village unveiling?" I asked angrily.

"What's this got to do with Langley?"

"I have a videotape that proves she was injured before she even got to city hall. She was in the car with Langley, Louie. I know she was."

Louie's mouth fell open. "Are you sure?" When I nodded he said, "Jesus."

"Did you tell this detective about my apartment?" I asked.

"No."

"Did you tell him it was Markbight?"

"I talked to him before I heard you mumbling."

"Did you tell him anything about Langley?"

"I only told him the bare basics."

"Good," I said. "Give me some slack on this one, Louie. Trust that I know what I'm doing."

And I knew too who I was after. When Louie went downstairs I dialed Harold Radisson's numbers in Clinton Falls and in Washington and left messages that we had to talk about his niece. I considered it a fifty-fifty chance that he'd return my call.

DETECTIVE-SERGEANT STEPHEN DELANEY of the Clinton Falls police department arrived around eleven. He was a short man with thick blond hair, a round, ruddy face, and a pugilist's nose. He was in his early fifties and wore a tailored white shirt and navy blue suit under an unbuttoned gray duffel coat that was spotted with rain. He sat down next to the bed, pulled a table closer, and set a spiral notebook and manila folder on it. He faced me, but his eyes didn't seem to focus on anything.

"Mr. Flanagan." He picked up a pencil and rolled it between his middle and index fingers. "You're better?"

"My head aches," I said.

"It will for another few days," Delaney said, "but the

pain'll pass." He fidgeted with the pencil. "As you can well imagine, Tom, Congressman and Dr. Radisson are gravely concerned about the safety of their niece."

"So am I," I said.

"I'm sure you are. You were with Miss Radisson?"

"Yes."

"Where?"

"At the university. In the penthouse of Indian Quad."

"Showing her the sights, were you?"

"We were talking. I thought it might be more interesting if we had our conversation there instead of at her apartment."

"Why?"

"I just did."

Delaney licked his lips and exhaled. "And what was the topic of your conversation?"

"Personal matters," I said laconically, "which probably have no bearing on your investigation."

Delaney sat for a moment, his eyes focused on the ceiling. Then he slammed his open palm on the table, breaking the pencil in two. He slid to the edge of the chair, his face reddening. "Whether or not these personal matters have anything to do with my investigation is for me and me alone to decide." Delaney sat back and started chewing a fingernail. A moment later he said, "I met your uncle Jack once."

"He worked with Louie."

"It was fifteen years ago when I was a patrolman. Someone burglarized a house they were renovating. He cooperated fully with our investigation." I opened my mouth to talk, but Delaney cut me off with a raised hand. "I also remember the day I heard about your parents and brother. It angered me more than anything. It still angers me. Let me say one thing, though, a piece of advice that I learned early on and that you as a historian might appreciate. You can never alter what happened, you can't reinvent the past. You can't change how your parents and brother died or what happened to the man who killed them. What happened is fact, Tom, cold, unforgiving fact. All you can do is move on."

We were silent for about thirty seconds. I was feeling renewed anger at the death of my parents and brother, but I was also thinking that what the Radissons did with Theodorick Crane proved wrong Delaney's musings about history.

Then he asked, "How long have you known Julianne?"

"About three weeks. She wanted to register for a course I'm teaching," I said.

"Did she?"

"No."

Delaney smiled crookedly. "No conflict of interest then. Lucky for you." He hesitated. "Your relations with the Radisson family are many and tangled, aren't they."

"My father supported Harold's run for Congress. Dr. Radisson was my advisor for a few semesters. And now I'm involved in the disappearance of their niece." Delaney didn't say anything, so I continued. "Louie told me you arrested Jens."

He nodded slowly. "At Harold Radisson's behest. When he told us his niece had disappeared, he demanded that we arrest your German friend and a few of his comrades."

"For what? Kidnapping?"

"He thinks the Clinton Falls Crusaders will do anything to derail the Patriot Village project."

"Even kidnap his niece? Do you really believe that?"

"Not really."

"Then why did you arrest him?"

"Because Harold Radisson demanded it," Delaney said. He smiled again and his lazy eye seemed to float. "I'm an honest cop, Tom, but not a stupid one. Had I refused to follow up on the cockamamie theory of New York's most powerful congressman, I'd be in the chief's doghouse for a long, long time. Don't worry, though, I think your friend and his group had nothing to do with Julianne's disappearance." Delaney produced another pencil from his shirt pocket, licked its tip, and set it on the table next to his notebook. "So you and Miss Radisson were talking."

"Yes. And then I was struck in the head. Some time later, I don't know when, I woke up in the back of a car. I was in pain and couldn't focus my eyes on anything, and I don't remember much except seeing Julianne in the front seat. Then the man hit me again. The next thing I knew I was here."

"Did the driver indicate where he was taking Julianne?"

"No."

"Was she tied up or gagged?"

"Neither."

"What did the driver say?"

"That I shouldn't have gotten involved."

"In what?"

"I don't know."

"Seems he was right," Delaney said. "Did you get a good look at the car?"

"No."

"The driver."

I shook my head.

"You didn't recognize his voice?"

"No."

Delaney hesitated before saying, "Who's Quincy Markbright?"

I tried to control my astonishment. "Who?"

"Quincy Markbright. Have you heard that name before?"

"Yes. He's Julianne's father."

"You found that out a few days ago."

"Yes."

"When Herr Erlenmeyer saw him in one of Louie's photos."

"Right."

"Louie must have photos of half the population of Clinton Falls behind that bar. And the other half in front of it."

"Detective, what's this got to do with Julianne's disappearance?" I asked, actually believing for a moment that he could read minds.

But then he said, "Jens Erlenmeyer mentioned Quincy Markbright when I brought up the Patriot Village demonstration. He claims it was Markbright who pointed him out to the police."

"He did mention that," I said as innocuously as I could.

Delaney sighed. "Is there anything else you know, Mr. Flanagan, that might help solve either case?"

"No."

"Maybe something someone else knows?"

"Pardon me?"

Delaney didn't answer. His eyes were focused somewhere on the ceiling when a puzzled look crossed his face and then disappeared. I concluded with relief that Jens had kept quiet about the videotape.

"Well, Tom. I spoke earlier about your involvement with the Radisson family. I certainly don't envy you," he said.

Delaney stood up and offered me a business card. I promised to call him if anything new came to mind. I was close to trusting him, but not close enough to tell him how tangled and extensive my connections with the Radisson family really were.

WHEN I GOT HOME that afternoon I saw that Louie's description of my apartment was no exaggeration. All the kitchen cupboards and drawers were empty; the shattered remains of plates, bowls, glasses, and coffee mugs were strewn about the countertop and kitchen table. In the bedroom the mattress and box springs were slashed, and stuffing and coils from them were buried underneath the clothes that had been thrown from my dresser drawers and closet. Other closets, too, were emptied of their contents: coats, shoes, blankets, board games, cereal boxes, and milk crates filled with old school work lay about the floor in piles. My robe, which Julianne was wearing when I left her on Monday morning, hung from a plastic hook on the back of my bedroom door.

I walked into the living room and saw that my couch too was torn apart. I saw that my television screen was smashed and my end tables and coffee table upended and scratched beyond repair. In the corner a file cabinet that contained all my important notes and papers was empty, the notes and papers nowhere to be seen. I was picking up stuff from the floor when I found a dozen family photographs and eight paintings from my mother's hand laying on the carpet in tattered piles. And then I saw my father's roll top desk, refinished with my help in the summer of 1979, smashed and splintered and rendered useless. I felt empty all of a sudden, as if my personal chamber of memory had been violated, ransacked, defiled. I found the phone underneath a pile of history books and old newspapers and called Mindy.

While I waited for her I found my Bible, opened it, and pointed.

> *A lion has come out of its lair;*
> *a destroyer of nations has set out.*
> *He has left his place*
> *to lay waste to your land.*
> *Your town will lie in ruins*
> *without inhabitants.*
> *So put on sackcloth,*
> *lament and wail,*
> *for the fierce anger of the LORD*
> *has not turned away from us.*

When I read the words from Jeremiah I thought of the shoving match Jens and I had had at Louie's, of the sex Julianne and I had shared a few nights before, of the anger I now felt towards the unknown man who had killed my parents and brother. What was I supposed to do with all the violence and hatred that had so recently invaded my life? Was there any way to expurgate it? To redeem myself and enter a state of forgiveness towards myself and others? I didn't know answers to any of these questions because I didn't know then whether the lion was an external enemy or had fed and grown on the malice that seemed to fill my soul.

Mindy arrived in ten minutes and stood motionless in the doorway, her mouth agape, staring at me as I sat sobbing amidst the detritus of my life. Then she dropped the wet umbrella she was holding, walked over to me, and offered me both her hands. I took them and stood up uneasily. I slipped my arms underneath her coat and wrapped them tightly around her body. More memories of Wednesday night came back to me, and my sadness and anger were placated not at all by the sweet scents of baby powder and rainwater.

"Let's get you over to my place," Mindy whispered after a few minutes. "We'll clean up tomorrow."

"I've got to see Whittaker," I said, stepping away from her. "I have to get Langley's notes."

"Theodorick Crane can wait . . . "

"It can't wait, Mindy," I said with a sweep of my arm. "One of the Radissons did this because they thought I had a set of Langley's notes. I don't know what's in them, but whatever it is must be important."

"Who did this?"

"Julianne's father, I suspect."

"How'd he get into your apartment, Tom?"

"With a spare key I gave to Julianne," I said with embarrassment.

ON THE WAY to the university I told Mindy about the videotape and about Wednesday night and about my own suspicions and tentative conclusions. She was dumbstruck, and then full of questions that I honestly could not answer.

Whittaker was in his office when Mindy and I arrived at

Hammond Hall. He took note of us, went back to his paperwork, and said, with out looking up, "Flanagan. McDonnell. Here on GOSH business?"

"I came to see Langley's notes," I said.

"Why?"

"I have reason to believe that Martha Radisson was in the car with him when it went off the road. They were arguing about Theodorick Crane and Cornflower that night. I think Langley knew something about her ancestor that she didn't want publicized."

Whittaker stopped writing and sat back. "So you know Martha was a Crane."

"Yes. Did you help her hide that?"

"She didn't need my help." He opened a drawer and took out a set of keys. "Why should I let you see Langley's notes? Especially since Dr. Radisson has been pressuring me to have them sealed?"

"Because I need to find the truth of how he died," I said. "Isn't that what we historians are here for? To find truth?"

"Lofty aspirations," Whittaker said. "We have a difficult enough time being heard at all. When we start prying into any accepted story, people accuse us of debunking and close their ears even more."

"Which is all the more reason for us to speak the truth," Mindy said. "The kind of cynicism you just expressed is what leads historians into parroting the politicians' lies."

"How deep into this are you?"

"Apparently getting deeper as we speak," Mindy said.

"And is truth your motive?"

"My motive, if I have one, is to help a friend." Mindy looked at me. "That's become clear these last few days."

"My advice, Mindy, is to stay out of it."

It was the first time I'd ever heard Whittaker use a Christian name.

"Langley's papers?" Mindy said.

Whittaker handed her the keys. I found the key to

Langley's office and looked it over. "For now, Mindy, you should stay out of it." I held up my hand before she could protest. "Remember when you asked me how well I knew Langley? I need to find that answer by myself."

I EMERGED FROM Langley's office several hours later, shaken by what I'd learned. I found Mindy in the TA office, absent-mindedly correcting a stack of multiple choice quizzes. I asked her where Whittaker was. She said he'd gone home an hour ago. I sat down and set one of Langley's notebooks on the table.

"We have to go to Louie's," I said.

"It's a bit late for a drink, Tom," Mindy said.

"I need to see a photo, Mindy. I think I know why Langley went to see Martha Radisson on the night of the accident."

"To ask about Theodorick Crane," Mindy said.

"And to ask about something much more important," I said, "and much closer to home."

Chapter Twelve

Most human beings operate like histori-
ans: they only recognize the nature of
their experience in retrospect.

—Eric Hobsbawm, *The Age of Empire*, 1987

A HALF HOUR LATER MINDY AND I WERE SITTING at the bar of
The 357. The neon lights were off, the front door was
locked, Louie looked exhausted. All was quiet save for the
hum of the refrigerators and the staccato drumbeat of rain
against the windows.

"Here you go, Tommy," Louie said as he handed me a
framed eight-by-ten photograph of a short, powerfully built
man and a thin woman with brown hair, both of them
dressed in corduroy pants and patterned sweaters. They
stood in front of a freshly painted Dutch colonial and next
to a sign that read "F & F Builders."

I flipped over the photo and said, "November 1975. Did
you know them well?"

"Well enough," Louie said. "Your uncle and I spent four
months renovating the house they'd just bought. It was one
of the grandest in the city, over on Lafayette Street. We gut-
ted the whole thing and started from scratch. New wiring,
plumbing, heating system, walls, floors, everything. Thousands of dollars worth of work. And you know what? They
lived there for two months, not even that, then sold the
house and moved to California."

I pointed to the woman in the photo standing next to Quincy Markbright. "And this is Helen Markbright, Harold Radisson's sister, as she looked in November 1975?"

"That's her," Louie said, "a week before Thanksgiving."

I handed her the photo. "Julianne's mother. Two months before Julianne was born."

Mindy looked at the photo then back at me, puzzled for a moment then astounded. "She's not pregnant. You mean Helen Markbright wasn't Julianne's mother?"

I set a volume of Langley's journals on the bar.

"This volume is from April 1975," I said, "written while Langley was in despair over the lack of progress he'd been making on his dissertation. The day after Garrett Hollister's body was unearthed Martha Radisson came to his apartment, shaken by the turn of events. Langley, who had already heard the news, invited her in. They spent the next four days together, just the two of them, talking, eating, drinking wine, making love, even planning a possible escape together to Bermuda or Canada. Langley wrote of their time together in terms of a dream, as something he had always longed for and, once it came, so wonderful as to be seemingly unreal.

"Then, on the fifth day, Langley asked Martha for Theodorick Crane's papers, which he believed would help him out of his intellectual rut. That broke the spell. That afternoon they got into a big argument, the decisive one for over twenty years as it turned out. Langley said he was certain that Crane was killed by someone other than a Federalist enemy. Martha was intransigent; she refused to give up the papers. Langley accused her and Harold of using him. She apologized for that, but explained again that sharing the documents was out of the question. Langley became angry and felt betrayed. He pressed her for an explanation. Martha refused to provide one. Within an hour she had gathered up her belongings and was gone. Langley wrote in his journal that he hoped to never see her again.

"Eight weeks later Langley received another visitor, Harold Radisson, who came to deliver some important pieces of news. The first was that Martha had taken ill and was staying with a family friend in Queens. The second was that he and Martha were getting married, for reasons, he explained vaguely, of expediency rather than love. Langley didn't understand this explanation until the first time he heard Harold use Theodorick Crane in a political campaign speech. Finally, Radisson informed Langley that he would soon donate a selection of Crane's papers to the State University at Clinton Falls, where Langley would begin teaching in September, and that he, Langley, would get first dibs at them. Harold emphasized that releasing the documents was a gesture of friendship that should not be taken lightly."

"And Langley finished his dissertation in December 1975," Mindy said.

"To his supreme dissatisfaction," I said, "since the documents Martha and Harold turned over were of little help."

"What does this have to do with Julianne?" Louie asked.

"She was born on January 7, 1976," I said. "That was seven months after Martha Crane disappeared and nine months after Martha Crane and Peter Langley spent four days together in his apartment." I alternated my gaze between Louie and Mindy as they absorbed and comprehended my words.

"My God," Louie finally said. "Did Langley know this?"

"Yes," I said. "But wait on that. First I want to tell you about Peter and Martha's continuing dispute. By 1980 Langley was recognized as one of the best teachers on campus. But he'd given up on research, which put him in a difficult position at a school that was completing its transformation from a top notch teaching college to a small but ambitious research university.

"Martha Radisson, having married Harold in a private ceremony in 1981, joined the faculty in 1982. She quickly established herself as the best fundraiser on campus. In 1987

Langley engineered the denial of her tenure, but thanks to Harold's influence it was only a delay, and it proved to be Langley's swan song. Martha landed the STARCH director-ship a couple years later and used her husband's political connections and her own smarts to turn it into one of the top research centers in the United States.

"In the '90s their conflict entered a cold war stage, with neither interfering much in the life of the other. In 1993 STARCH received a grant from IBM to put a large selection of its documents online. And Langley's talent as a teacher continued to improve. In 1994 he received the Distin-guished Teaching Award, the prestige of which was lessened somewhat by his remaining an associate professor, earning $41,000 per year compared to Martha Radisson's $75,000."

"Didn't Toby Reynolds work on that IBM project?" Mindy asked.

"Thanks for reminding me," I said. "Toby found a pack-et of correspondence that proved John Coffey couldn't have killed Theodorick Crane."

"For the political reasons we talked about?" Mindy asked.

"Sort of," I said. "It was true that the Federalists had no intention of killing Crane. But that wasn't the problem."

"What was?"

"Joseph Crane said his father's throat had been slashed from right to left, from behind. He even demonstrated the fact in front of the judge with Coffey's own knife. But cut-ting from right to left was impossible for Coffey because he'd lost three fingers on his left hand in a hunting accident a year before Crane's assassination."

"Toby told Langley this?"

"Immediately. He also agreed to smuggle the documents out of STARCH. But before he could get them out, Martha Radisson got ahold of them, hid them somewhere, and pun-ished Toby by blacklisting him."

"Did Langley have another possible explanation?" Mindy asked.

"He did," I said. "He believed that the Republicans themselves killed Crane to keep him from disrupting their power base."

"His own party?" Mindy said in disbelief.

I nodded.

"What about Julianne?" Louie asked.

"She came to Clinton Falls soon after Christmas, having guessed correctly that Martha was her benefactor. Quincy Markbright followed her here, probably because he was getting money too and didn't want to lose it because of something Julianne might do."

I produced the most recent volume of Langley's journal. "Langley's diary tells the story. Markbright visited Langley the second day he was in town. He explained that Julianne was looking for information on an Iroquois woman named Cornflower who was executed by Theodorick Crane and whose ghost haunted Julianne's dreams. Langley, knowing that Harold Radisson had appropriated Crane as his ancestor, asked why no one had told Julianne that Crane wasn't really her ancestor. Markbright's reply was that Crane *was* Julianne's ancestor because she was, by birth, Martha's daughter, adopted by him and his wife soon after the birth. Langley asked how old she was. Markbright told him she was born on January 7, 1976."

"And all Langley had to do was the math," Louie said.

"Yes. Later that day Langley read through his own journals and searched his memory and found what he knew was the truth. He drove to Markbright's hotel and questioned him again about Julianne's parentage. Markbright insisted that she was Harold and Martha's child, born on January 7, 1976 at Columbia Presbyterian Hospital in New York City and given to him and his wife Helen the following day. Markbright assured Langley that he had seen Martha Crane in her hospital bed, recovering from a complicated and traumatic birth.

"This was in late December. Mindy, it was later that day that Alexa found Langley so disoriented."

"No wonder," Mindy said.

"He agonized over what to do and waited with apprehension for Julianne's visit. But she never showed, and he finally confronted Martha Radisson with his knowledge. They were driving out to Crane's End, possibly to talk with Julianne, when the car went off the road and into Westcott Creek."

I paused and opened the journal. "Langley was going through one of the most difficult times of his life. His epilepsy had gotten worse, the Bucci affair was weighing heavily on him, and then he had a serious attack on the night Alexa visited his office. Then Julianne and Quincy Markbright came to town and made matters even worse.

"The last three entries are dated the ninth, twelfth, and thirteenth of January. On the ninth his thoughts returned to Theodorick Crane. If only Martha hadn't lied at the outset. If only she'd chosen him over Harold. If only she'd shared Crane's story, if only he'd been able to tell it: if any of these had come to pass he was sure he could have succeeded in changing the world. On the twelfth he called his lawyer to see if he could be legally recognized as Julianne's father. And on the thirteenth he wrote this:

" 'I've waited for the girl's visit as if I were anxiously awaiting the millennium. The visions are even there, but whether they're brought about by epilepsy or the phenobarbital or by some deity or devil, I do not know. Twenty-seven years of uncertainty is about to end—whatever happens tonight there will be a culmination. The political imperative of knowing and telling Crane's story is gone, but I must know it and tell it now to destroy the Radissons. Or destroy them by revealing Julianne's identity. Either way the girl— my daughter!—will be my instrument. And my salvation.' "

I TOSSED AND TURNED on Mindy's couch that night, replaying

again and again the words I had read in Langley's journals. Finally, a little after five, I went home and started cleaning up the mess in my kitchen. I was nervous and disoriented, the muscles in my abdomen like a coil wound too tight and ready to snap. I couldn't help thinking about Julianne, about how I'd fallen under her spell and how she'd used me and betrayed my confidence. But I was angry with myself for allowing it all to happen, and burned off my frustration with hard physical work.

As I was dragging furniture out from the living room to my apartment building dumpster, my thoughts returned to the Jeremiah passage I'd read a few days before. I'd never been keen on seeing God as a vengeful deity, but given the events of the past nine months I had to wonder if that's where the roots of my suffering lie. Am I a target of God's wrath? Had my own behavior so angered God that He had released the lion of destruction into my life? How much worse would things get? For a brief moment I thought about Mindy and Jens and how they were being pulled into the mess that was mine. For an even briefer moment I considered abandoning my quest for truth lest the lion devour them as it was surely devouring me. But I was driven by righteousness and hubris in equal measure, and from that morning on I knew that neither lion nor deity would stop me short of death.

I had the living room cleaned up and was half way through with the bedroom when, covered with sweat, I received the phone call I had been hoping for and dreading at the same time. It was Harold Radisson, and he wanted to talk, at noon, in his downtown office.

"I'm not coming to your office," I said.

"Why not?"

"I want to meet on neutral turf. Otherwise, forget about meeting at all."

"Where then?" he asked, annoyed at my refusal to play by his rules.

"Theodorick Crane's old haunt. Fort Montgomery."

"In weather like this?" he said.

I looked out the window. "The rain bothers you?"

"It's not me I'm worried about, Tom."

"Meet me at the northeast casement. Twelve o'clock." I hung up the phone before he could reply.

I grated and fried some potatoes, took a quick shower, and dressed in a pair of khakis, a blue Henley, and heavy work boots. After cleaning and putting away the dishes I sat down at the kitchen table and wrote a long letter to Delaney explaining what I knew and suspected about Martha Radisson's involvement in Langley's accident and Quincy Markbright's involvement in the Patriot Village demonstration. I called Jens, who had been released from police custody the previous evening, told him where Radisson and I were meeting, and told him to be there, out of sight, by noon. Then I put on my raincoat and dropped off the letter and the Patriot Village videotape at Mindy's with the instructions to deliver them to the police station at two o'clock that afternoon. Then I drove downtown.

I had come to believe in my years in academia that important revelations are had, missing links found, and crucial discoveries made only as a result of hard work and diligence, by poring over page after page of tedious, often unbearable material in search of valuable clues or bits of information. Dr. McNally had put it this way: in the bedrock of the printed page, just waiting for the dogged among us to chisel them out, lie buried the priceless diamonds of information that make all academic pursuits worthwhile. But I had learned through experience that things just as often happen by accident, happenstance, good fortune, God's grace, that, with good fortune, nuggets of truth and awareness can fall into our laps like gold pouring off a rainbow into a leprechaun's pot.

I was fortunate that afternoon when I decided for no apparent reason to approach Fort Montgomery indirectly from the west. My half hour drive took me across the Mohawk, along the south shore of the river past a growing ice jam at the raised lock, and down a half-dozen one way streets through the shadowy maze of boarded up, crumbling buildings that once comprised the city's bustling textile district. As I rolled through a stop sign and turned right onto Ferry Street I almost sideswiped Quincy Markbright's silver Dodge, which was parked alongside an especially run down brick monolith next to the old Ostend hat factory. I stopped my car, got out, and examined the interior of Markbright's car to see if I recognized it from Wednesday night. Then, seeing it was almost twelve o'clock, I drove to Fort Montgomery, not quite sure of what to do about Markbright's, and probably Julianne's, proximity.

I parked on Maiden Lane and entered the national monument area through a gate to the left of the gift shop. I walked across the parade ground, at times on a muddy path and at times through various depths of snow, entered the northeast casement, and ascended the steep stairs to the bastion. Shielded somewhat from the rain by the wall of the battlement, I put my hands in my coat pockets and gazed out at the snow on the ground below and the dark ribbon of river beyond.

Harold Radisson walked up the stairs a moment later, wearing dark brown leather boots, wool pants, and a long tan coat that he'd left unbuttoned. He was tall and lean. His collar length brown hair, combed straight back and set into place with styling gel, was unaffected by the steady southwest wind and rain. His eyes were like blue lasers. He got right to the point.

"You should have heeded my wife's warnings, Tom."

"The truth is more important than Dr. Radisson's threats, sir."

"You're a persistent man, Tom. I admire that quality. I admired it in your father. Unfortunately, you apply that persistence to an enterprise that goes directly against both my interests and my ambitions."

"Let me tell you three things," I said, trying to disguise my fear with conviction. "I know through a set of Langley's diaries that he and Dr. Radisson spent an entire week together right after Garrett Hollister's body was unearthed. I know through those same diaries that Langley met with Quincy Markbright a few days before he died. And I saw a videotape of the Patriot Village demonstration that shows Dr. Radisson was injured well before the incendiary hit. The tape also shows you unwrapping a bandage from around her head." Radisson bit his lip and was silent, so I continued. "I want to know the connection between these facts and Peter Langley's death, sir. I want to know the truth."

Harold Radisson stuffed his gloved hands into his pockets and tried to atomize my courage with his eyes. "What are you getting at?"

"Markbright told Langley that Julianne's real parents were you and Dr. Radisson. But Langley knew that he had spent nearly a week with Martha nine months before Julianne was born. He finally asked your wife about it on the night of January thirteenth, most likely while driving together out to Crane's End. That's when they were injured, your wife seriously and Langley fatally."

Radisson hesitated for a moment then pulled his right hand out of his pocket and made a motion akin to that of dribbling a basketball. "I came here to warn you one last time before you really get hurt," he said. "But I decided to also give you a glimpse into the origins of Julianne Radisson. Think of it as a reward for your persistence. Think of it as a favor for the son of a good friend. Then please, for your own good, forget about all this. Write your dissertation. Get a job. Leave Julianne and her family alone."

He leaned up against the parapet and began to speak, not once releasing me from his gaze. "I was in New York when Hollister's body was found, otherwise Peter and Martha never would've spent that time together and this confusion never would've happened. But Martha was terribly afraid, and I wasn't around for her. Peter was. So they resumed the fling they'd had going just before we started our string of burglaries. It was a stupid move on her part, but it happened.

"We found out she was pregnant about six weeks later. There was no question the child was Langley's. We considered our options and decided to put the baby up for adoption. So we moved to Manhattan, where Martha could give birth anonymously, more or less, and away from Peter.

"Then, seven and a half months into her pregnancy, the problems began. Premature contractions, the flu, pneumonia. In late December Martha was rushed to Columbia Presbyterian. The doctor, himself just a kid, had no idea what to do. He induced labor, augmented it, and finally performed a c-section on the morning of January seventh. The baby was surprisingly healthy given what it had been through. But it was touch and go with Martha. She was unconscious for three days and barely aware for three more after coming to.

"I'd spent most of my time making arrangements for the baby. I didn't want a blind adoption because I didn't trust our social services to place the child in a good enough home. So I contacted my sister and her husband, who'd been trying for years to have their own child, and made them an offer: they take the baby as their child, move far away from upstate New York, and promise to keep the child's identity a secret from Martha. In return I agreed to pay them ten thousand dollars a year in perpetuity.

"What a mistake that turned out to be! They took Julianne to Los Angeles. They quickly proved to be as incompetent as a set of parents can be. They were drunk most of the time and they treated the poor girl like an unwanted doll. Then they tried to make it up to her by spoiling her beyond redemption. Finally, just before Julianne arrived here to investigate this ridiculous curse, I wrote the letter I should have written a decade ago. I told Markbright I was cutting off his money because he'd failed me as a friend and Julianne as a father. The idiot responded by coming to Clinton Falls to try to extort money from me."

Radisson paused for a moment, frowned, and shook his head in what might have been sadness. Then his expression cleared and he continued. "You're probably wondering why I never told Martha. At first I was going to, but then I began thinking about possible scenarios: Martha suing for custody, showing up at the Markbrights' doorstep with a gun and demanding her baby back, you never know. I decided early on it was best for my wife to remain ignorant of the situation. So the day after the birth, as Martha lay unconscious, I accused the doctor of malpractice. I told him that he should've performed the cesarean at the outset and that his hesitation may yet cost Martha her life. I threatened to sue the hospital. I could tell my threat had teeth because the doctor was visibly frightened."

Radisson laughed softly. "That afternoon I had in my hand a certificate documenting the birth of a healthy baby girl to Quincy and Helen Markbright. When Martha came to, fortunate for us the day after Quincy and Helen took Julianne home, the doctor told her, with sadness just dripping from his face, that he was terribly sorry to inform her that the baby was a stillborn. Then he gave me the papers to prove it."

I considered Radisson's story for a moment and looked him right in the eye. "What's preventing me from telling all this to your wife?"

"Nothing. In fact, you telling her won't make a bit of difference. My sister Helen told her all about it when she brought Julianne to Clinton Falls for our mother's funeral. Martha set up a trust fund for Julianne, but agreed to keep her maternity a secret."

Did she know Langley was the father?"

"Of course."

"And he told her he knew all this on the night he died."

"He knew it because Markbright told him. When he told Martha about it in the car she began striking him in the arms and head. He lost control of the car as he tried to fend off her blows. The rest is ancient history."

The wind picked up and the rain started falling harder. I could feel my bile rise into my chest. "Why did Markbright throw the incendiary?" I asked.

"Martha's injuries needed an explanation. It was her idea. I reluctantly agreed. I paid him twenty thousand dollars in cash to do it and leave town. Once again he failed me."

"But the unveiling was four nights after the accident."

"Martha . . . how should I put it . . . kept her injuries fresh. She used anticoagulants among other things and even reopened a few of the cuts on the night of the unveiling. She suffered bravely through the pain."

I wiped a combination of rain and sweat from my eyes. "And you tried to complete the cover-up by blaming Jens and the Crusaders. The truth of all this will ruin your career."

"And Peter Langley's reputation, and Ben Fries's life," Radisson said without missing a beat. He saw my eyes widen and he smiled, and then took a few steps towards me. "You heard me right, Tom. I called the state police right after I got off the phone with you, and I promise you that Mr. Hartman or Fries or whatever he's calling himself these days will be behind bars within the hour."

"You're a cruel man, Mr. Radisson."

"I'm a realistic man, Tom, able to see and understand what's truly important in the world and then act on it."

"At any cost?"

"At any cost."

I felt significantly colder all of a sudden and didn't know how to respond to a man who considered his own lies more valuable than the truth. A man my father had admired.

"I've got an idea, Tom," he said in a soft voice that nevertheless pierced my ears like a shout. "Why don't you come to Washington and work for me? Take the career path you should have taken years ago. You can go a long way down that path."

I walked away, intent on finding Markbright and Julianne.

"Or work for me here if you prefer. I need people like you in my campaigns. I need people with moxie. I think that's what your father would've wanted."

I turned around to face him and felt the coil in my abdomen tighten. I clenched my fists in my pockets and saw him draw back his lips into a vicious smile. If his words and expression were meant to provoke they worked. I made as if to walk away then took my hands out of my pockets and charged right at him.

He was ready for me. He grabbed my arm as I delivered a left cross and used my own momentum to drive me to the floor. I landed face first with my arms out and palms open. I could feel the cold, hard wood tear into my skin. I rose to a knee, but Radisson knocked me down again with a kick to my lower back that sent shocks of pain in every direction.

He bent over me and spoke into my ear. "If you know Crane's story, Tom, be wise and keep it to yourself. If you don't know it yet, be smart and don't try to learn it. Don't try to be like Langley." Then he stood up and said, "No more warnings," and gave me one final kick to the ribs.

JENS HELPED ME UP a few minutes later.

"Thanks for being here," I said sarcastically.

"I couldn't find the place," he said.

I turned around and thrust my hands into a pile of snow. "Did Radisson see you?" I asked.

"No."

"Listen, Jens," I said. "Markbright is in a warehouse a few blocks away. I think he has Julianne with him."

"Where?"

"On Ferry Street. Near the corner of Maiden Lane."

Jens looked back towards the fort's entrance, hesitated for a moment, then ran away before I remembered that Markbright had a gun.

I limped to the warehouse and found them on the second floor in one of the few rooms with its windows intact and some furniture still in place. Markbright had Julianne gagged and tied up to a fold-out cot. He sat in a lawn chair reading the Sunday paper, with a revolver resting on his knee. A kerosene heater burned between them, and rain dripped from numerous holes in three of the room's four corners.

I stopped at the top stair and looked at Julianne. Her face was streaked with dirt and tears and her hair was dull and flat. The sleeve of her coat was torn from the cuff up to the elbow. At that moment I felt she deserved everything Markbright had done to her.

Then I saw Jens burst through a doorway on the other side of the room. Markbright moved quickly when he saw him, grabbing the revolver, aiming, firing. The bullet stopped Jens's forward motion, and he jerked back as if hitting his left shoulder against a doorjamb. He fell to the ground in a spasm and clutched his arm in an attempt to stop the flowing blood.

Markbright turned the gun on me as I moved forward and hollered for him to stop. I saw him pull back the hammer again, and I stopped walking and held up my arms.

"Don't shoot," I said. "I just want to talk." I looked at Jens. "We have to get an ambulance in here."

Markbright didn't respond and seemed to put pressure on the trigger.

I moved slowly towards Jens, who was groaning now and clutching his arm harder. "I don't want to take your daughter away from you," I said. "Harold and Martha are the ones in trouble, Quincy, not you."

I kneeled down beside Jens and told Markbright what I was going to do so he wouldn't get startled and fire the gun again. Then I took off my raincoat and Henley, both of them spotted with melted snow and dirt and my own blood, ripped off a shirt sleeve, and tied it around Jens' wound. Getting back into my coat I looked down at Jens, and then back at Markbright.

"You charged him, Jens. He shot the gun in self defense," I said.

Jens' eyes grew large with incredulity and anger. "No such thing . . . " he said in a whisper that even I could barely hear.

"Self defense, right Jens?" I said, willing him to agree.

He looked at me for a moment then began to lift his head. I placed my hand behind it to help him. Then, with a tremendous effort, he spoke. "It was self defense, Markbright."

With that Quincy Markbright lowered the gun. "I can't believe you're here, Flanagan. You must have a death wish or something."

"Testify that throwing the bomb was Harold and Martha's idea. Between that and what happened to Langley we can get them on conspiracy charges. Then there'll be nothing standing in the way of you and Julianne."

"She's my daughter, Flanagan, I raised her. And I deserve the money Harold promised me to do it." With that Julianne turned towards him, her eyes wide.

"What were you looking for in my apartment?" I asked.

"Langley's notes."

"Why?"

"To see what else he knew about Theodorick Crane."

Back to Crane, I thought. "What exactly?"

"He had a copy of Joseph Crane's memoirs," Markbright said. "The ones written by Joseph himself right after his father's death, the ones that tell the truth."

"Langley has it? Where?"

"Had, Flanagan. Past tense. He gave it to me on the night we met." Markbright half smiled and shook his head. "He thought it was worthless. He thought Joseph Crane had gone mad with his talk of Cornflower's ghost. He was so obsessed with the other story, with the Crane and Radisson family lie, that he couldn't see the truth even though it was staring him right in the face."

"What are you talking about?"

"I told him that Crane's murder had nothing to do with politics. I told him how Joseph Crane had invented the myth of a political assassination to cover up the real story behind his father's murder. I told him how the myth had been made history by generations of Cranes from Joseph on. He didn't listen to me because he wanted so badly to believe the myth. He gave me Joseph Crane's memoirs, thinking they were useless."

"The political murder was a myth?" I said. "You mean to tell me that Cornflower's ghost really did commit the murder?" I looked at Julianne, who was sobbing, her face turned to the ground.

"Listen, Flanagan," he said with a wave of the gun. But he stopped short when he heard the sound of sirens approaching the building from Maiden Lane. He moved to the window and looked out, his eyes wide with panic. He looked at me, at Julianne, back at me, then shoved the gun into an inside coat pocket and ran.

"What did you find in his notes?" I asked, thinking about Julianne's story. But Markbright was gone by time the words left my mouth. I walked over to Julianne, untied her, and tore the gag away from her face.

She winced and then opened her mouth wide and took a deep breath. Her face was flushed and she was sweating heavily. "Get me out of here," she said.

I had to keep myself from hitting her. "Why should I?"

"Please, Tom, take me away before Uncle Harold gets here."

"What was Markbright talking about?"

She looked at me for a long moment. There was fear in

her eyes, the kind no one could fake. "Uncle Harold kidnapped me, then turned me over to my father and demanded that he take me back to California. But my father's not going back because he wants money that Uncle Harold won't give him."

"Your uncle kidnapped you? He was the one who hit me?"

"The first time, yes. Then he and my father carried you to my father's car. Then we went to your apartment."

"Tell me about Crane, Julianne."

"I can't, Tom. I won't."

"You owe me."

"I know, I know." She wiped her forehead with the palm of her hand. "Look, I won't tell you about Crane, but if you get me out of here I promise I'll tell you about Langley."

I was close to telling Julianne the true nature of her relationship with Langley when I heard Jens groan behind me. "We can't leave him here," I said.

"He'll be fine. Your tourniquet stopped the bleeding." We both looked out the window and saw the police cars coming near. Behind the first cruiser was Harold Radisson's Mercedes. "For God's sake, come on." Julianne ran out the same door Markbright had, then turned around with a pleading look on her face. "Come on!"

I knelt down beside Jens and foolishly and at great risk to him told him to lie still until the police arrived. Then I caught up with Julianne and we ran through the back of the building and around another and to my car parked on Maiden Lane. As we pulled away I could hear over the rain and Julianne's crying the distinct sound of three gunshots, whether from Markbright, the police, or both, I did not know.

Chapter Thirteen

When they turn the pages of history,
When these days have passed long ago,
Will they read of us with sadness
For the seeds that we let grow?

—Neil Peart (Rush), "A Farewell to Kings," 1977

"YOU'RE TELLING ME THAT HAROLD RADDISON'S WIFE was involved in Dr. Langley's car accident? That Quincy Markbright threw the incendiary?" Stephen Delaney was furious and demanded the entire story. I told him some of it, the part he'd already read in my typed statement that Mindy had delivered to him earlier that afternoon. "Why the hell didn't you tell me all this before, Tom?"

It was a little after four on Monday afternoon, and we were sitting at a small folding table in Delaney's office. The rain was falling hard against the window. The adjacent hallway bustled with activity as uniformed officers and public safety officials dealt with the growing number of storm and flood related problems, mostly fallen tree limbs, downed wires, backed up sewers, and flooded streets.

"I couldn't tell you," I said. "I had to find out the truth on my own. I was trying to vindicate Langley."

"Vindicate him for what?"

"From being blamed for the crash. I know he didn't drink."

"Do you have any proof?"

"He had epilepsy. He didn't drink."

"Do you have any concrete proof that he hadn't been drinking on the night of the accident?"

"No."

Delaney scowled and leapt out of the chair, causing it to fall backwards to the floor. Then he got on the telephone and ordered a subordinate to get him the Patriot Village videotape that was part of my package, the audio tape of all 911 calls from the night of January thirteenth, and all the police and medical paperwork dealing with Langley's accident. He clicked his fingernails on the telephone as he listened to something, maybe silence, on the other end of the line. After a moment of this he shouted, "Right now, goddamit!" and slammed the handset down.

He sat down in another chair without picking up the one he had knocked to the floor. "Why'd you come to me now?"

"I realized this afternoon that I'd lost control of the situation," I said. "I need help." I didn't add that I'd also become afraid of Harold Radisson—Jeremiah's Lion—and the injury I knew he was capable of inflicting. Yet I still had sense enough to realize that maybe even the police couldn't protect me from that.

"Tell me what happened at the warehouse."

"I walked into the room just as Markbright pulled out a gun and shot Jens in the arm. As I was helping Jens, Markbright heard the police sirens and fled. I untied Julianne and she ran away too, muttering something about wanting to keep away from her uncle Harold."

"You didn't follow her?"

"I'd hurt my ankle back at Fort Montgomery. I couldn't keep up. So I went back to my car and drove home."

Just then a fluorescent ceiling light flickered, causing both Delaney and I to pause and look up. I took it as a warning from on high to circumscribe my half-truths.

"Why was she afraid of her uncle?" Delaney said.

"She said he wanted to hurt her. She didn't elaborate."

"Do you know where she is?"

I lied again and told him I didn't.

"Louie's right about you," Delaney said. He stood up and walked out of the room, leaving me to figure out alone what he, and Louie, meant.

Delaney returned to the room an hour later with a video and audio cassettes in one hand and some manila folders in the other. He dropped both bundles on the table, where they landed simultaneously with a sharp crash.

"An ambulance delivered Quincy Markbright to the hospital after he tried to play Jesse James with two of our best officers. He suffered a gunshot wound to the chest. He's not going to make it. I had a conversation with him, Tom. He said Harold Radisson was the one who struck you and abducted Julianne. He said Radisson turned Julianne over to him and ordered him to take her back to California. But why? Why? What did she know?" Delaney removed the video from its cardboard sleeve. Then he walked over to the VCR and inserted the tape, his good eye alight with anger. "We're going over this tape now. Then I want you gone."

He worked the pause and rewind buttons on the remote control as we watched the video. I was too shocked at the news of Markbright to pay much attention. When I finally looked at the monitor I saw that the image was distorted by tracking lines. This made Delaney even more irritated than he had been before. He pressed the stop and eject buttons, grabbed the tape out of the machine, and flung it aside.

"See Gus Malinowski at the university AV department," I said. "He'll play the tape for you on a high quality machine."

"I will," he replied curtly.

"What's Jens' status in your investigation?"

"If your story about Langley's accident and the demonstration proves true, your friend is exonerated."

"Can I go now?" I asked. "I want to visit him."

"Go," Delaney instructed with a wave of his hand. "And tell him I'll be over to talk."

I STOPPED HOME to clean up and change, and grabbed my mail on the way into my apartment. Most of it was the usual junk—an advertisement for the new wholesale club opening on the other side of town, a solicitation for a Clinton Falls Alumni Association Visa even though I wasn't an alumnus yet—but one letter, postmarked February 12 from Grand Manan, New Brunswick, caught my attention. I tore open the envelope and read the letter by the gray light of the window, and read it again and again until my eyes burned and the light grew too dim for reading.

> *Tom,*
>
> *Needless to say your visit took me by surprise. As pleased as I was to see you, though, I cannot say the same thing about your traveling companion. I don't trust that girl, Tom; I don't trust any of the Radissons. It didn't take me long to conclude that staying on Wellesley Island would be dangerous. Don't think it's your fault. I'd prepared myself for such an eventuality long ago, and in truth expected it to come much sooner than it did. The Bay of Fundy is a good place, just as beautiful as the Saint Lawrence River and an excellent place to hide. And there's more than enough work to do.*
>
> *Informing you about my situation is the secondary reason for this letter. I write to tell you something about your father that, given the purpose of your visit, I think you should know.*
>
> *I mentioned that your mother was a regular contributor to Preserve the Islands. She was also a good friend who would confide in me when she needed to talk, most often during the week when your father was away working on his newspaper.*

Our friendship was clandestine, of course, and completely non-sexual.

She came to see me one day in July 1985, in tears because she and your father were having financial troubles and were being forced to sell the cottage. I had heard rumors to this effect from some of our neighbors, but I didn't know the details until your mother told it to me that day.

You know your father was a devoted and influential supporter of Harold Radisson. When it came to the news he was also devoted to the truth and to his reporters, even after selling a controlling interest in his paper in 1983. A few weeks before your mother's visit one of your father's junior reporters, Frederick Teed, had come to him with evidence that one of Harold Radisson's wealthiest financial backers, H. Paul Gass, was neck deep in fraudulent loans and shady real estate deals, many of which financed some of the largest building projects in the area. Your father liked Teed's work, but wanted more evidence and more background information. He gave Teed an expense account to pay for more research and promised him a raise and promotion when the exposé was published later that year.

Somehow Radisson found out about the story. He came to your father's office a few days after Teed did and asked your father as a friend to not print it. Your father refused. The next day he and Teed were called into the office of the chairman of the board of Northeast Communications, Inc., the corporation that now owned a controlling interest in the paper. Harold Radisson was there, as was H. Paul Gass and a pack of lawyers from his bank. The corporate chairman—I can't recall his name, but I do know that he's currently serving time for insider trading—gave your father a choice of either withholding publication of the article or surrendering his shares in the paper and losing his job. Without hesitation he chose the latter, and both he and Teed were fired on the spot. But Teed refused to turn over his research and interview notes, and went on to write for

Mother Jones, *where he published his information a year
later as part of a larger investigation of the savings and loan
scandal.*

*You and your brother never heard this story because your
father was afraid you'd consider him a failure for losing his
job and a coward for not fighting back. Your mother was
certain that his silence was eating him alive. And he did try
to fight back—your mother showed me articles he'd written
but was unable to publish attacking Harold Radisson.*

*Your father knew about my life as Albert Hartman,
Tom. As a newspaper man, it would have been difficult for
him not to know. He didn't broadcast the knowledge, but
only because I was more valuable to him free rather than in
jail. I certainly paid a high price for that freedom.*

*When I get settled here I'll write again, with a return
address. I want to know how things are resolved.*

> *Sincerely,*
> *Ben Fries*

I TOOK A QUICK, HOT SHOWER, dressed in a pair of khakis and a
dark blue shirt, and drove to Wildwood to see Jens.

I drove in a trance that took me back a dozen years to
the time right after my father lost the paper. My father's silence was eating him alive, Ben said, and thinking back I remember how he did indeed withdraw, from my mother,
from Patrick and me, from everyone except a few friends at
the Elk's Club and Jimmy's Tavern. But I was soon off to
college, and his bad moods, witnessed by me only on
Christmas breaks, seemed nothing more serious than a common case of the holiday blues.

I found Jens sitting up in bed with no shirt on, his
shoulder heavily bandaged, his arm in a sling. He was
watching a hockey game on television and actually looked
happy.

"This is the third time I've been shot at," he said cheerfully, "and the first I've been hit."

"Third time?" I said as I sat down in a chair next to the bed.

"The first was a rally against neo-Nazis that I attended in Heidelberg—I think I've told you about it—and the second was during an armed robbery of a jewelry store."

"You robbed a jewelry store?"

Jens laughed and then grabbed his arm in pain. "I was in the jewelry store buying a necklace for a girlfriend when it got robbed." Then he added, soberly, "To tell you the truth, Tom, this time I feel fortunate to be alive."

"I gave Delaney the tape, Jens. He knows all about Langley's accident and Markbright's involvement in the demonstration."

"Then I am finally proven innocent?"

"Yes."

"Thank you," he said. He held out a hand for me to shake, a gesture I didn't expect. Then after a moment he said, "I'm worried about you. One thing I have learned as an activist is how to achieve results by taking protest to the edge of recklessness without actually going over that edge."

"Am I getting reckless?"

"You got beat up last week and again today, and had Quincy Markbright fired at you he might not have missed."

"Do you remember what Danton said in September 1792 as the Austrian and Prussian armies were closing in on Paris?"

"Ah, yes. 'We must vanquish them with boldness, always boldness, and still more boldness. Only then will France be saved.' "

"Substitute 'Langley's reputation' for 'France' and you might understand."

"Boldness in the face of danger is one thing, Tom. Recklessness in attacking the Radissons is quite another."

I gave him a long look. "Is your concern genuine or self-serving?"

"What do you mean?"

"I think there's one particular Radisson you want me to stay away from."

"She is moving out of both our reaches," Jens said. "What is your objective, Tom?"

"To salvage Langley's reputation," I said.

"From what?"

"From charges of professional misconduct, from the shame of having died the way people think he died, from the insult of having the passion of his life hidden from him . . . "

"The passion of his life?"

"It's a long story." But Jens' expression said tell it, and my own thoughts were turning back to my father, territory into which I didn't want to go, so I sat down and told it. "Theodorick Crane. In the early seventies, Harold and Martha Raddison and Langley stole most of Crane's papers from various archives throughout the state. Langley never got to see or use most of the documents because Harold and Martha discovered a family secret in them that they didn't want to go public."

"I thought Crane's story is in Langley's dissertation."

"Part of it is. Eventually, Harold donated all Crane's papers having to do with the revolution to the university. But the family secret concerns events after the revolution. It has something to do with Theodorick Crane's murder."

"So Crane was murdered," Jens said.

"In 1800, while plotting a revolt against the ruling eastern New York oligarchy."

"Really!" Jens' eyes opened wide. "Who killed him?"

"The Radissons say it was a Federalist enemy, but Langley thought it was a Republican." I paused. "And Juli-anne, of course, thinks he was killed by a ghost."

Jens thought for a moment. "How personal is this, Tom?"

"What?"

"Mindy and I have discussed your involvement at length. We feel you're trying to solve the problem of Langley's death because you're having a difficult time dealing with your parents' death."

Somewhere, deep inside my own consciousness, I knew there was a kernel of truth to this. But I'd never admit it, not to myself and especially not to Jens. "Langley died an incomplete man, Jens. He never fulfilled either his dream or his potential. All because of Martha and Harold Radisson."

"We all leave loose ends, Tom."

"I know, but . . . "

I broke off the sentence when I saw Stephen Delaney walking down the hallway towards Jens' room, a manila folder in one hand and a tape recorder in the other. He wore a troubled look on his face.

"I just finished reading the paperwork on Langley's accident," Delaney said as he entered the room. "Then I made a call to the coroner to see if he could provide any more information. Did you know Langley was taking barbiturates for his epilepsy?" Delaney opened his notebook and flipped through a few pages. "Phenobarbital. That's heavy stuff."

"That's right," I said. "He mentioned phenobarbital in one of his last diary entries." I stood up. "That night with Alexa. She said he'd been drinking. He'd probably injected just before she came to his office. Jens, she mistook his reaction to the drug for drunkenness."

Delaney shook his head. "Sorry to say, Tom, that the girl was probably right about the drinking. On the night of his accident Langley had lethal amounts of both barbiturates and alcohol in his system. If the crash didn't kill him, that combination certainly would've."

"Why didn't we know about this? Why wasn't there an inquest?" I said.

Delaney turned to another page in his notebook. "Langley's death was classified accidental at the request of —get this—Harold Radisson and the university president."

"And you agreed?"

"Whoa, Tom. I wasn't the investigating officer on the case. I didn't know of any of this until now."

"Radisson didn't want an investigation," I said, turning away.

"According to the coroner, the university president made the request in person. He said he wanted to keep Langley's drug use quiet for the same reason Langley himself did while he was alive, to avoid a scandal. As for Radisson, I suspect, like you do, Tom, that he wanted to keep people from asking questions. My guess is that Radisson engineered the entire thing."

Then Delaney held up the tape recorder and placed a finger on the play button. "Things get even more interesting," he said, locking onto my eyes. "Tell me if you recognize this voice."

He pressed the button, and out of the speaker came two female voices: the steady, controlled one of the 911 operator, trying as best she could to control the situation, and the quavering, frightened voice of the young woman who made the call: "There's been an accident, a terrible one, on Route 5. Yes, just west of Westcott Road. Only one car. I saw it go off the road. An emergency? Yes, it's an emergency." Then the unmistakable voice of Julianne Radisson faltered, and there was a crash as the phone hit the floor.

"I promise to have her at Louie's in an hour," I said, breaking under the pressure of Delaney's gaze. "But please let me talk to her first."

Chapter Fourteen

If we need another past so badly, is it inconceivable that we might discover one, that we might even invent one?

—Van Wyck Brooks, *On Creating a Useable Past*, 1918

IT WAS STILL RAINING WHEN I LEFT WILDWOOD, harder than it had been earlier that day or all the day before. The rain fell in sheets, often propelled sideways by a strong southwest wind, and at times I thought the dirty snow banks at the sides of the road were shrinking before my eyes.

I stopped by The 357 to tell Louie what was going on. I knew something was wrong when I walked into the bar and saw him serving customers without his usual bartender smile. When he saw me he flipped a damp towel onto his shoulder and motioned for me to follow him into the kitchen.

"Mindy's upstairs with Julianne," he said angrily. "She brought her here after not being able to get in touch with you."

"I was just going to pick them up."

"For Christ's sake, Tommy, Mindy walked out of her bathroom and found Julianne standing in the kitchen with a knife in her hand. She's taking care of her. She made her tea. You shouldn't have taken her to Mindy. You should have taken her to Delaney."

"I couldn't do that Louie. She's terrified of being turned over to her uncle. She's afraid he'll hurt her."

"That's all the more reason Delaney should handle it."

I turned around without answering and ran upstairs. I found them in the living room, side by side on the couch. Julianne sat with her head in her hands, wet from a combination of rain and tears. Mindy, still in her raincoat, was rubbing Julianne's back and shoulders, comforting her as best she could. Mindy looked up when she heard me walk in.

"Is she OK?" I asked quietly.

"Does she look OK?"

I pulled up a chair and faced them. "Julianne, we need to have a serious talk."

"Does it have to be now?" Mindy said with a glare.

I ignored Mindy and reached forward with a tissue to wipe Julianne's cheek. "Quincy Markbright is in critical condition at Wildwood. He fired at a police officer and the officer shot back. The doctors aren't giving him much of a chance."

Julianne's head drooped forward.

"And I just heard the 911 tape from Langley's accident. You called it in, Julianne. You were there. Detective Delaney is on his way here to talk about that. Before he gets here I need to know what you saw."

Mindy started to protest, but Julianne cut her off.

"It's all right, Mindy," she said as she lifted her head and wiped her eyes with the back of her hands. "I promised Tom I'd tell him."

She took a breath and told her story. "I was waiting outside the Humanities building a few hours after I caught Aunt Martha and Professor Langley arguing. I was supposed to pick up Aunt Martha and drive her to the garage. I was sitting there in my car, listening to the radio, when Aunt Martha and Professor Langley walked out of the building and got into a taxi. So I followed them. The taxi dropped them off at a brownstone a few blocks away from campus—"

"Langley's house," I interrupted.

"Yes, it must have been. They got out of the taxi and into another car parked behind the building. A brown Acura." Julianne raised her bloodshot eyes to meet mine.

"Langley's car," I said anxiously. "Who drove?"

"Aunt Martha drove. And she drove fast. Too fast for the freezing weather. They were almost to Crane's End, about a half mile away, when she missed the turn onto Westcott Road and slid on the ice. It was horrible, the sight of the car smashing through the guard rail and rolling over. And it was so sudden." Julianne started crying again.

"They didn't see you tailing them?" Mindy asked.

"I wasn't right behind them," Julianne said between sobs. "I didn't have to be because I knew exactly where they were going. When I got to the turn I stopped my car and made my way down to the creek. It was so dark and so cold. I must have fallen a dozen times. I found Aunt Martha halfway out the car door and Professor Langley in the passenger side slumped forward, his head just a few inches away from a tree branch that had gone through the windshield. The back window was shattered. There was glass everywhere. There was blood everywhere, too, most of it Professor Langley's. And there was a gun in the front seat next to his hand.

"I stood there for I don't know how long and just stared at the wreckage. I was so frightened. Then Aunt Martha opened her eyes and whispered for me to come near. She said she couldn't be found in the car with Langley. She told me to help her get to Crane's End. So I helped her. I somehow managed to get her out of the wreckage and walk her home. It was the longest half mile I've ever walked."

"And you left Langley lying there?" I said.

Julianne shook her head. "Uncle Harold was home for a Patriot Village news conference. He surprised me; I didn't expect him to be there. When I told him what was happening he said that everything I'd seen had to be kept secret. He grabbed me and kept shaking me and telling me this as if I wouldn't understand. He started walking around the house, muttering, trying to figure out some way to make it look like Professor Langley had been in the car alone. Then, after we cleaned up Aunt Martha and got her into bed, Uncle Harold ran out of the house and went to the car.

"He was half crazy when he returned. He was ranting on about Professor Langley's statement and how it would ruin him if he didn't get hold of it. When he finally calmed down he said he had an idea. He gave me a bottle of vodka and ordered me to make Professor Langley drink it. But I was so tired and weak that I couldn't do it. I just sat there, holding the bottle. Uncle Harold was furious. He hit me and called me a useless brat. He grabbed the bottle from my hands and took it himself to the car. He was gone for about twenty minutes. He came back with the gun but without the bottle."

Julianne paused and breathed deeply. "I went back to the car because I had to see if I could help Professor Langley. I found him still alive, but in the driver's seat now. Uncle Harold had moved him over and cleared away the footprints and any other evidence that anyone else was at the scene. What else he did was terrible.

"I can still hear Langley groaning, struggling to breath. I can see the mixture of saliva, blood, and vodka dripping from his mouth, and his broken arm hanging bent and limp against his side. I remember being cold again all of a sudden and shivering uncontrollably. It was so quiet and still. There was no sound, no movement, nothing to distract me from the cold and from Langley's quiet moaning. All I wanted was to get out of there, to get back home. I regretted even going back to the car.

"Then I heard him say something in a voice so faint that I wasn't sure he'd actually spoken. I leaned into the car and put my ear right next to his mouth. He told me . . . he said an attack was coming. I didn't know of what. But he was afraid, he felt it coming and was afraid. He told me exactly what to do, and I followed his instructions. I went around the other side of the car and took a leather case out of the glove compartment. I opened the case and found two syringes inside. I don't know what was in them, some kind of whitish, opaque solution. I walked back to the driver's side and held his head upright so I could hear him speak. Then I took each syringe and injected the contents into his abdomen. He opened his eyes and looked at me, and I could see the light in them fade away. I heard him whisper again. He asked me to take off his glove. It was a difficult thing to do because his hand was so stiff from the cold. When I got it off he reached up and touched my cheek . . ." Julianne mimicked the gesture as her words trailed off.

Then she said, "I left him there and went back to Crane's End and called 911. The police came to the house about half an hour later. I told them again what I'd told the 911 operator. Uncle Harold didn't know about it because he was with Aunt Martha in a bedroom on the third floor." When Julianne finished talking she bit her lower lip and slowly shook her head, tears rolling down her face and neck.

"What did you do with the syringes and the leather case?" I asked.

"I took them back to Crane's End and threw them in the trash."

I laid my hand over Julianne's, yet looked at Mindy. "Those syringes contained a barbiturate solution that Langley took to control his epilepsy."

"I'm sorry, Tom. God, I'm sorry."

"Did Langley say anything about Theodorick Crane?" I asked. "Did he know how he died? Did you tell him?"

Julianne raised her head and looked at me with wet and hollow eyes. "It all comes back to him, doesn't it? Him and Cornflower. They've been dead for two hundred years, but not quite dead because they seem to destroy anyone unfortunate enough to become drawn into their orbit." She wiped her eyes with the back of her hand. "Yes, Tom, Professor Langley did say something about Theodorick Crane, or rather something about his daughter. He knew about her, Tom. He said her story was in the statement he wrote, the one my uncle was looking for but couldn't find."

I stared at her for a moment, my heart racing, then said, "He wasn't talking about Crane's daughter, Julianne . . ."

"Tom!" Mindy said suddenly, her eyes alight.

Just then I heard a door slam and heard someone ascending the back stairs to Louie's apartment. I recalled what Quincy Markbright had said about the least likely story being the true one. "Who killed Crane, Julianne?"

"You can't know," she said. "You don't want to know."

Julianne began to sob again as Delaney entered the room and produced a notebook from his rain-drenched coat. Mindy put her arm around Julianne and drew her near. I left the room, my anger and frustration growing exponentially but still under control.

Mindy joined me in the hallway a moment later, her hands shaking and lower lip trembling. From where we stood we could see Julianne and Detective Delaney talking on the couch, and could hear Delaney asking Julianne if she was ready to go.

"The detective's taking her in," Mindy said. Then she looked at me with an expression of shock on her face. "You can't tell her that Langley's her father, Tom."

I didn't respond.

"Does this detective know about that?" Mindy said.

"No," I said as I buttoned up my coat. "Can you go to the police station with her? Stay with her, Mindy?"

"Yes," she said. "Where are you going?"

"To find Martha Radisson. I have to tell her what her husband did. And I have to find out what happened to Theodorick Crane."

"Be careful, Tom," she said, taking my hand for a second and then letting it slip away.

I RAN DOWN THE BACK STAIRS, grabbed my hat and coat off a hallway hook, and set off to the university despite the radio's warnings that water was rising across half the city.

My car's wipers worked furiously against the rain as I sped down Monroe Avenue, the only person foolish or desperate enough to be on the road. Puddles had become miniature lakes, their depths impossible to gauge in the rain-blackened night. My car lurched and chugged as I hit the deep ones too fast. It finally stalled in a sea of water underneath the Thruway.

I opened the door and stuck out my foot with the expectation of touching pavement. I was at first puzzled and then frightened by the sensation of water swirling around my ankles and flowing into the car. I lost my footing in that moment of confusion and fell out of the car into knee deep water. But when I stood up I could see pavement twenty or so yards ahead, and after a few minutes of slippery wading I ascended out of the water onto dry land. Only a few days afterward did I realize that it was at that same spot—the Thruway underpass, about four blocks from my own apartment—that I had first felt the painful needles of cold on the opening day of the semester.

And like that day I soon found myself standing in front of a locked door on campus. I walked around the Administration building and looked up at Martha Radisson's office, the only illuminated one on the third floor. I was soaked to the skin and had my hands cupped like shields above and around my eyes, but with little effect. Over the sound of water rushing beneath the huge iron grate at my feet I heard someone walk out the main entrance to my left. I ran towards the door, slipped on the wet cobblestone, and fell again. I was cursing loudly when I felt myself being helped to my feet.

"A bad night to be locked out of a building," said the university president. "Are you hurt?"

I kept my head down and face hidden. "No, I'm fine. Is there a telephone in this building? My car broke down. I need to call a tow truck."

"Use my cell phone."

"No thanks. I mean, I also have to use the men's room."

"I see. Yes there is a telephone. In the basement." He took out a ring of keys, unlocked the door, and held it open for me as I walked through. "Turn right at the bottom of the stairs. And good luck."

I thanked him and said goodnight, and waited for him to pull away before ascending to the third floor.

I found Martha Radisson in her office, looking down at a pile of thick cardboard and metal boxes that were stacked on her desk. I walked through the door without knocking.

"What are you doing?" I asked breathlessly.

She held up outstretched arms and then let them drop to her side. "Theodorick Crane's life, Tom. This is why we're here."

"Where was all this stuff?"

"STARCH has a storage room in the tunnels that no one but me knows about. I carried these boxes up here when I realized how hard it was raining."

I stared at the boxes, and for just a second wanted to pull out a match and light them on fire. "Joseph Crane's memoirs?" I asked.

"Those volumes are at Crane's End. What you see here is a carefully arranged selection of documents that I put together with the intention of finding them if anyone pressed too hard for the rest of Crane's story. There are some interesting revolutionary war documents, some of them explaining Cornflower's death. There's enough here to satisfy most appetites." She continued, "I'm leaving, Tom. Whittaker and the university president were just here. We agreed that it would be best for me to turn STARCH over to Professor Batcher."

"Julianne?" I asked.

"She's coming with me. We're leaving town tonight."

"Have you heard about Markbright?" I asked.

"No," she said.

"He's been shot. He's dying."

"Good."

I swallowed hard. "Your husband kidnapped Julianne and ordered Markbright to take her back to California."

She stopped packing and stood motionless, gazing out the window. Then she reached into one of the open boxes and pulled out a small notebook, its leather cover dry and cracked from time. As she slowly flipped through its pages a few confetti-like pieces of yellow-brown paper broke off and fell to the floor. She turned back towards the window, the notebook still in her hand. "Harold didn't want her to know about Theodorick Crane. He was afraid that she'd publicize it, or at least tell you. The heartless son of a bitch threatened to implicate Julianne in Langley's death if I told her Crane's story. We argued about it for weeks before I told her anyway. Harold panicked, something I'd never seen him do before. I told him that all Quincy wanted was money. I told him to give it to him. He didn't listen."

"I thought you were behind it," I said. "Julianne called you that night."

"Harold had the phones of Crane's End tapped. The phones in his own home! He didn't trust me. He was determined to monitor my dealings with Julianne and interfere if necessary."

"Markbright thought you wanted to take Julianne away from him."

Martha's eyes lit up. "Take her away? How about get her back? She's my daughter, Tom. Harold took her away from me over twenty-one years ago."

"I know, Martha. I read a set of Langley's diaries that explain almost everything. Your husband filled in the blanks."

"For years Harold and I were foolish to think we could keep our lives and Julianne's life and Theodorick Crane's death hidden. The only difference now is that I realize how impossible it is. My husband still doesn't."

"Julianne is with Detective Delaney right now telling him about Langley's accident."

"I just talked with the detective as well. Peter's death is another thing we can't keep hidden."

I looked again at the boxes. "Tell me about Joseph Crane's memoirs. Did Joseph reveal his father's murderer? Was it really a Republican?"

She shook her head and sneered as if she were growing impatient with an especially thick-headed freshman. "You're as unimaginative as Peter," she said.

"What do you mean?"

"Can't you see? Can't you understand the trick that bitch Clio has played on us? Crane, like Peter, died at the hands of his daughter."

I grabbed Martha by the shoulders and made her face me.

"There was no Joseph Crane," she whispered in my ear, "at least not until 1804 when Josephine Strong and Antoine Radisson invented him."

I stepped back from her in shock, her weary smile the only response to my bafflement.

Chapter Fifteen

Historic truths our guardian chiefs proclaim,
Their worth, their actions, and their deathless fame;
Admiring crowds their life-touch'd forms behold
In breathing canvass, or in sculptur'd gold.

—Joel Barlow, *The Prospect of Peace*, 1778

WHAT FOLLOWS IS THE CRANE FAMILY STORY, pieced together from what Martha told me that evening and from the one journal and few dozen pages of correspondence that survived the night's events.

In 1762 the four-year-old Mary Strong was placed in a Kingston, Ontario orphanage run by Georges and Josephine Radisson, he of French and she of mixed British and Huron descent, both of them Catholic. Their oldest son, Antoine, was the same age as Mary, and the two children grew up as brother and sister.

In 1777, the same year Antoine left Kingston to enroll in a Paris seminary, Mary Strong left Kingston to join the American war effort. She took up residence with the Seneca, and eventually persuaded chief Blacksnake to lay aside his objections and give her letters of introduction to a few of his more important patriot contacts in New York State. It was at this point that she took the name Cornflower to reestablish her ties with the Iroquois.

She met Theodorick Crane in 1778 as he recuperated on his farm from the injuries he'd received in Cherry Valley.

She came to him with a simple request: re-enlist in the Continental Army, join the upcoming Sullivan expedition into Central and western New York, and deliver papers detailing the strength of British forces to a contact she had on Sullivan's staff. Crane, whose wife and children were in Albany, agreed because he trusted Mary Strong and because he fell in love with her the minute he saw her.

He didn't know that her request was a ruse. In truth she was growing increasingly concerned about the destructive impact the impending expedition would have on the Iroquois. What she really wanted from Crane, and from the other American officers she enlisted, was information on American strengths and marching orders that she could relay to the Iroquois. She didn't consider herself a turncoat. She insisted that she'd resume serving the Americans when the expedition was over and the danger to her people had passed.

The results of her work exceeded her expectations. She obtained information from Crane and the others and passed it on to the Iroquois, who evacuated their villages before Sullivan's advance scouts arrived. True, massive quantities of foodstuffs and huge tracts of farmland were destroyed by Sullivan's army, but only a few Iroquois were captured by the patriots and even fewer were killed in battle. Her principle goal of saving human lives had been accomplished.

Sometime during the expedition Crane and Cornflower became lovers. Soon after it ended she discovered that she was pregnant. She returned to Ontario, where she gave birth to a baby girl named Josephine Strong, in August 1780. Then, in October, leaving the child in the Radissons' care, she journeyed across the Saint Lawrence and down through the Adirondacks with every intention of resuming her work as an American agent and of telling Theodorick about the child.

She arrived at an Oneida settlement outside present day Utica in late November, intending to stay only a few nights and continue on to Fort Montgomery, where, she had been told, Theodorick Crane was commander. While there she became involved in a dispute between British and American sympathizers over which side, if either, the tribe should support. Mary Strong was instrumental in swaying the decision in favor of the Americans.

But in January 1781 the village was attacked by a band of pro-British Iroquois led by Joseph Brandt. Cornflower was one of the hundred and fifty survivors, and the next day, while the villager's houses and fields smoldered, she organized them and led them southeast to Fort Montgomery, where she hoped Crane would provide food, shelter and medicine.

She didn't know that Crane and his men were suffering through privations as bad as those she and her band of refugees were trying to endure. In a year's time Fort Montgomery had become a pit of disease and human misery, ill supplied and all but forgotten by the Continental Congress once the main theater of war had shifted to the south. One third of Crane's men had died of dysentery or consumption or some other undocumented malady; the rest survived without adequate food, clothing or fresh water. The men at Fort Montgomery had nothing to give the Oneida refugees, even if they'd been willing to help.

And they were not, because Theodorick Crane had discovered her treachery of two years before and had vowed to hunt her down and kill her. When the refugees arrived at the fort on February 10, 1781, Crane had Cornflower arrested and sent the rest away. She admitted everything, but tried to convince Crane that her actions were for the greater good. But Crane didn't buy it, and the next morning he executed Cornflower and two unnamed accomplices. The official record, found in Martha Radisson's secret stash of documents, said that Crane, "on February 11, 1781, dutifully put to death three Iroquois enemies of the American Republic." Crane's journal, in the same document collection, reports that the bodies were burned on a pyre at noon that same day. There's no mention of any vow of vengeance made by Cornflower, but Crane was deeply disturbed by the deaths of his daughters and wife within two years, and wondered in his journal whether "supernatural influences" were involved.

In 1793 Antoine Radisson returned to North America. His ostensible reason for coming back was to sell his father's estate in Kingston, which had been willed to Antoine when both his parents died in 1792. His trip had another purpose, though, which he concealed from almost everyone he knew: to garner American support for the French in their war against the British. He'd given up his priesthood for a seat in the French National Assembly, had become a revolutionary crusader, and when he received word that he had business to attend to in Canada he took it upon himself to proselytize for the French Revolution in the United States. He met Theodorick Crane in the summer of 1793 at a session of the New York legislature. Crane proclaimed himself a natural and dependable ally, not only against the British themselves but against British sympathizers in America as well.

Antoine Radisson did not know that Crane had executed the woman who'd been raised as his sister until he finally made his trip to Kingston in 1799. He met Josephine Strong there, a young woman of nineteen years who had become obsessed with her mother's death and with the circumstances that surrounded it. Also, like many of the Iroquois who had settled along the north shore of the Saint Lawrence River after the war, she despised the American government and blamed it for the rapid decline in her people's fortunes. She'd long since decided to murder Crane, out of personal vengeance and as a payback for the destruction wrought by the American army. Radisson was horrified by Josephine's plan, but his attempts at discouraging her from following through on it met with no success.

Josephine visited Crane numerous times in December 1799 and January 1800, dressed in Indian clothing, presenting herself as the resurrected Cornflower. Her visits drove Crane into a state of delirium. He was wracked with guilt over the deed he had committed nineteen years before. For weeks he secluded himself on his farm, seeing no one. He was unable to eat or sleep. He lived in fear. He wrote of committing suicide. Then, on February 11, 1800, the nineteenth anniversary of her mother's execution, Josephine Strong struck.

Theodorick was in bed when Josephine entered his room just after nightfall. She sat down at her father's bedside and comforted him. Then she filled a tub with hot water and helped him into it. They talked about his time in the army and about his frustration at not being able to provide for his men at Fort Montgomery. When he lamented the lack of appreciation that young men currently showed the previous generation's heroes, she assured her father that his deeds were not, nor ever would be, forgotten. She calmed him, bathed him, and then offered him wine that she had laced with a mild poison. He accepted the wine, drank it, and after a few minutes fell asleep. Then Josephine Strong slit her father's throat, from right to left as Joseph Crane's memoirs asserted. She opened all the windows and left him there. His corpse was found three days later, a prisoner of frozen blood and ice.

Josephine returned to Kingston, herself driven close to madness by the emotional and psychological trauma of having committed the act. For weeks she actually believed that she was Cornflower's ghost. It was in this state of mind that she told the tale, from Cornflower's point of view, in a journal that the Crane family knew about but didn't understand. It became the source of the Radisson family ghost story, was mistaken by Langley as the "elusive, incomplete and unreliable" memoirs of Joseph Crane, and was in

Langley's possession until he gave it to Quincy Markbright just before Christmas.

Meanwhile, as Josephine recovered, the circumstances of Antoine Radisson's life changed dramatically. Already under suspicion for his earlier propaganda work in America, Radisson became a declared enemy of the British government in April 1800. He went into hiding on the American side of the Saint Lawrence when his land in Kingston was confiscated and a warrant issued for his arrest. He appealed to the French Canadian authorities for help, but they, Catholics with no sympathy for a man who had abandoned the Catholic Church and had embraced its revolutionary enemy, refused.

Radisson hoped to return to France, but there, too, he was out of favor after another turn in the revolutionary tide. Early in 1801 he received news from a political associate that First Consul Bonaparte had drawn up a list of public enemies that included many radicals, Radisson among them. His friend, who had escaped to Switzerland, assured him that he'd be imprisoned if he returned to France. His options thus limited, Radisson devised his own scheme by which he and Josephine Strong would cover up her part in Theodorick Crane's murder and draw mutual benefit from it.

Josephine, posing as "Joseph Crane," made her first public appearance in Clinton Falls in October 1803. Early the next year "Joseph Crane" pointed a finger of accusation at John Coffey, a loud, garrulous, hard drinking Federalist who had gotten himself killed in a duel two years earlier. The accusation was plausible enough given the contentious political climate in Clinton Falls. With the help of fraudulent evidence, a sympathetic lawyer, and Antoine Radisson's testimony that Coffey had threatened Crane's life on numerous occasions from 1794 on, a jury delivered a quick postmortem conviction. The falsified story of the murder investigation and trial is told in another document known as

Joseph Crane's memoirs, written by Josephine Strong and Antoine Radisson in 1804 and 1805. This was the document discovered and then hidden away by Hiram Crane in the 1870s and re-discovered and kept under wraps by Martha Crane and Harold Radisson in the 1970s.

In May 1804 "Joseph Crane" sold his Clinton Falls farm to Clarence Radisson, Antoine's cousin and Harold's genuine ancestor. Antoine Radisson and Josephine Strong married and moved to an isolated farm near Elmira. The marriage happened on one condition: Josephine's insistence that they change their and their children's surnames to Crane so that their progeny would never forget Theodorick's crime.

Josephine died in 1831, and grief fell down upon Antoine like rain. It was obvious to his close friends and to his four children that he was a broken man without his wife of twenty-seven years. He began to reflect upon his life, to reconsider his actions, to repent. He spent his last year writing the true story of his and Josephine's lives. He mailed the memoir to his cousin Clarence in Clinton Falls, where it ended up buried and unread in the Radisson family papers until Martha Crane found it in 1975.

"Who knew about it?" I asked after Martha had finished telling me of the third and final memoirs' existence.

"No one. That's always been the most astonishing thing of all to me. Harold insists that his family was completely ignorant of it. My family, of course, knew nothing of it. I might have been the first person since 1831 to lay eyes upon it."

"How did you find it?"

"It was blind luck. I was in Clinton Falls researching an unrelated topic a week before Garrett Hollister's body was found—the week Julianne was conceived. I was astounded when I read it. I made photocopies, and Harold and I stole it after I told him the true story."

"What about Markbright? He knew something because

he told Langley that the ghost story was closer to the truth than the political one."

"Quincy knew through Harold that the political tale was fraudulent. But he didn't know about the 1831 memoir, which meant that the ghost story was the only one left for him to believe. Moreover, the last several entries in Theodorick Crane's journals describe the visits of Cornflower's ghost. It wasn't Cornflower, of course, it was Josephine Strong, but Crane didn't know that, and his diary seems to support the ghost story."

"Did Langley read Theodorick Crane's diaries?"

"Yes. But he dismissed them out of hand as the ravings of a very disturbed man who knew that his political career was over and that his life was in danger. And to be fair, it took me five years to understand their true meaning. Until I found Antoine Radisson's memoir I believed, like Peter, that Crane's murderer had a political motive. Until then Crane's last few diary entries were a piece of the puzzle that refused to fit."

After a moment's silence I said, "What happened that night with Langley, Martha?"

She turned towards me with a slightly opened mouth and then turned back around. As I moved closer I could see in the window the reflection of an emotionally wracked face, sullen and empty, beyond tears.

"Mr. Flanagan, I—"

Her telephone interrupted her, as it had during our first meeting a couple of weeks before. But this time I could hear Harold Radisson on the other end and I could tell from his voice and from the shadow of shock and fear that crossed Martha's face exactly what the call was about. I had my coat on and was helping Martha on with hers when she told me that the first floor of Crane's End was submerged under five feet of rapidly rising water.

MARTHA RADISSON DESCRIBED the events of Peter Langley's final night alive as we traveled west on Route 5 averaging between twenty and twenty-five miles per hour, both of us cold and wet and more than a little frightened.

"I thought Peter had come to my office to ask once again for Theodorick Crane's papers. Before he had the chance to speak I told him that he wasn't getting them. He cut me off and told me that he'd found out about Julianne. He was angrier than I'd ever seen him. I backed down and told him the truth about our daughter.

"What were we to do? There we were, enemies and rivals, confronting the secrets of our past yet unable to provide each other an ounce of solace or comfort. Have you ever had the feeling that God was totally absent from a situation, Tom? That it's just you and whoever else is there and nothing else besides the failures and tragedies that make up our lives? That's how I felt at that moment, and for a few minutes I knew exactly why Peter was an atheist. I'd even forgotten that Julianne was waiting in her car outside, waiting to drive me to the garage."

I thought back to the moment that Louie told me about my parent's and brother's death. I didn't admit to Martha that in that moment, but only for a moment, I did indeed share her lack of faith. "What happened next?" I asked.

"Peter demanded the documents in exchange for his silence on Julianne's true identity. I agreed, and we drove to Crane's End. But on the way there I had a change of heart. I thought about how different Peter was from the time I first knew him. How he'd become someone I didn't recognize, someone I didn't want to know."

"What do you mean?"

"He'd hardened himself into some odd species of disillusioned rebel, Tom. He was angry and bitter, cutting himself off from everything that once mattered to him. As we approached Crane's End my resolution grew. By the time we reached Westcott Road I became determined that this man would reveal neither Crane's story nor Julianne's identity."

"That's not true about Langley, Martha. I read his diaries."

She pounded the steering wheel with a fist. "And what did they say? Was he still willing to make the sacrifices that Albert made? Was he still willing to commit himself to true reform? Did he still believe in progress, like he believed in it when I first knew him? He'd given up, Tom. He'd lost faith in humanity long before he'd lost his faith in God. He used his classroom as a hiding place from the world, protecting himself with his lectures from the real dangers that Harold and I encountered every day."

"He hadn't given up!" I said. "He taught me all I know."

"You don't even know about you! I could have guided you through the Ivy League and into an academic post more prestigious than you could imagine. Peter was fond of saying that you were the brightest star in the department's sky, which was true before your luster faded. Peter was determined to keep you by his side. Didn't you realize that? Couldn't you see that you were his trophy, stolen from me and paraded in front of me to boost his own ego? You were his only real victory, Tom. He refused to let you slip away. It was because of him, because of his refusal to set you free, that you faded."

"I wouldn't have changed a thing," I said, doubting my own words as I spoke them.

But Martha didn't respond because by this point we had reached the intersection of Route 5 and Westcott Road. I wasn't paying attention to the road, and I lurched forward when, seeing that the bridge ahead had washed out, she hit the brakes hard.

"Is this where it happened?" I asked with my heart pounding as the car slid to a stop.

"Yes," she said quietly. "He had a gun with him. He was ready to use it if I reneged on my promise to hand over the documents." She hesitated for a moment and put her head against the top of the steering wheel. "I was driving Peter's

car because he'd had an attack. I told him to take his medication but he refused because he wanted to stay alert. I'm
sure that his refusal made his second attack, the one he
suffered in Julianne's presence, even worse. He was pressing
the gun against my ribs as I drove. I was about to make the
turn onto Westcott Road when I lost control of the car. It
happened in a flash. I might have been going too fast, I
might not have been. I still don't understand."

Martha paused and caught her breath. "I loved him,
Tom. I've always loved him despite what he'd let himself
become. I hate myself for what I did . . ." Her voice trailed
off into quiet weeping.

"Did you at least tell him who killed Theodorick Crane?"
I asked.

Martha nodded, then hardened her jaw and shot me a
sudden look that, in the strange yellow light that filled the
car's interior, sent a shiver down my spine. "I also told him
that Josephine Strong, in her madness after the murder,
vowed to destroy anyone unfortunate enough to love or be
loved by a Crane."

SILENT AND STUNNED, I helped Martha out of the car and
across what remained of the bridge's stone supports. Then
we joined hands and waded through a muddy maze of fallen
and half-submerged tree limbs, somehow managing to stay
on the pavement and off the treacherous, rapidly eroding
ground.

I wondered what it was like in other areas of the city.
Was Fort Montgomery inundated? City hall? I had seen only
one other flood in my years in Clinton Falls, in 1989 when
April rains and snow melt overflowed the river and submerged a few city streets and back yards. The Mohawk was
a popular attraction that spring, harmless entertainment because people knew that the foot or so of water that flowed
into basements along the river could be drained by a hard-
working sump pump.

But this flood was different: because it was out of season, because it came upon us so quickly, because it was so severe, and because, at that moment, it seemed to concentrate its fury on Crane's End—the Radisson home—and the secrets inside. I recalled another prophetic verse that I'd run across before, this time from Amos: "But let justice roll on like a river, righteousness like a never-failing stream!" Was I to be devoured by Jeremiah's lion or drowned in Amos' river of righteousness? I didn't know, but I was determined as we approached Crane's End to face either destiny as a true and just punishment.

The house itself seemed to glow against the dark backdrop of the rainy night, and I could see its chopped up reflection in the waters that surrounded it. The water got deeper and more agitated as Martha and I approached the house and the angry river beyond, too deep for either of us to touch ground. So we swam against the swirling current for the last fifty or so yards and continued swimming through the portico and through the open front door. Then we climbed onto the main stairway, water dripping from our bodies, both of us weary and shivering from a wet cold that soaked through our clothes and burned our skin.

Harold heard us enter and ran from a second floor room to the top of the stairway. "Thank God you're safe," he said to Martha, taking her by the hands.

"Let go of me," she said, jerking away. Then, "What did you do to Julianne?"

"Nothing, Martha. Neither Quincy nor I touched her."

"She looked pretty bad when I last saw her," I said.

"Stay out of this, Tom." Harold Radisson said.

I ignored him. "Markbright was shot by a police officer. He told Stephen Delaney about throwing the incendiary and about what you did to Julianne."

"And Julianne told Delaney about the accident," Martha said. Then she glanced back at the water and her eyes widened. She returned her gaze to Harold, whose face had gone white. "Where are the papers?" she asked.

Harold produced from his coat pocket a bound volume similar to the one Martha had held in her office. "This was the only one I could salvage."

Martha climbed the stairs and snatched the notebook from her husband's hand. She hurriedly flipped through its pages. "This is the wrong one! I promised to give Julianne the 1831 diary!"

"The water rose too quickly," Harold said. "I didn't have time to save the other volumes."

Martha glared at her husband. "I didn't see your car outside. Is it under water? You've been here all day, haven't you? Waiting here to keep me out of the basement."

"It's better this way, Martha. Now no one will ever know."

"It's about time that everyone does know," she said. Then she slapped him across the face with the leather notebook, tossed it up the stairs, and turned around and dove into the water.

Harold rushed to stop her, but the slap had stunned and slowed him. Martha was already gone, around the corner and through the doorway and into the kitchen. Harold jumped into the water in pursuit.

I followed. I was a good swimmer from all the practice I'd had on the river, but I still found it difficult navigating my way through the hallway and into the kitchen and around the many objects that floated and bobbed in the swirling brown water. Harold was well ahead of me, maybe, like Martha, already through the basement doorway. But I wasn't about to go down there, so I found the countertop, steadied myself against it, and lifted my head out of the water to take in air and get my bearings. The river was gushing with a roar through the broken windows and rising to the ceiling, which I judged to be ten feet from the floor. Neither Martha nor Harold was anywhere to be seen.

I'd been in this position for about a minute when the water near the basement doorway bubbled and swirled, and
Harold Radisson emerged from it, gasping for air. He tried
to speak, but could only manage a few monosyllabic utter-
ances: "Too deep, too dark . . . must have . . . where . . .
can't find . . . oh, God . . . can't find . . . what?" I saw him
go under again, obviously not by choice, and I swam hurriedly over to him, the veins in my head throbbing as I tried
to make sense of his fractured words. I didn't find him in
the spot where he had gone down, so I dove into the murk
with the certain knowledge that I was plunging to my own
death.

The water was dark and fraught with obstacles, with
small pieces of furniture and kitchen utensils, with chairs,
cutting boards, and one or two small electric appliances. I
felt lucky that none of the debris struck me in the head. As I
moved to my right against a powerful vortex of water I
slammed into Harold Radisson, his eyes open and his arms
slowly flailing as if he were clumsily performing an under-
water aerobics routine. I felt my way down his body and
found his leg solidly wedged at the ankle between the wall
and basement railing. I pushed and pulled on his foot, but
couldn't move it an inch.

Suddenly I felt myself being pulled away from him. When
I turned my head I saw Martha further down the basement
stairway clutching my ankle. I drifted down to her level,
thinking that she too was stuck, and was surprised and confused when she vigorously shook her head and in one burst
of movement propelled herself past me and up to the sur-
face. I quickly caught up to her, my lungs about to burst,
and I saw that she too was in serious trouble from having
taken in water. I took hold of her and somehow managed to
lift her head far enough out of the water for her to breathe.

But no breath came, and I knew I couldn't hold this position long enough to drain the water from her lungs. I could
sense the coming of death upon her, and I didn't know what

to do. I thought about Harold and shuddered. What was I to do about him? The failing strength of my arms was the only thing keeping Martha from sinking back into the water and drowning. There was no way I could save her and also free her husband from the railing. I recalled Ben Fries's letter and thought about my father. I thought about Langley lying helpless in the front seat of his car. I remember thinking about forgiveness and mercy, and prayed for Harold's soul.

Then I was hit in the left leg by an object being propelled upward from the basement: a long, flat piece of wood, heavy but afloat in the current, that I identified as a leaf from a dining room table. Dazed, realizing that this was Martha's last chance for survival and possibly my own, I grabbed the piece of wood and wrapped Martha's arms around it and my arms around her. Then, using all the strength that remained in my right leg and despite a searing pain in my left leg, I pushed us along the kitchen walls, out into the hallway, and up the stairs.

I rolled Martha onto the landing and felt a slight pulse. I started mouth-to-mouth respiration, blowing slow, deep breaths into her lungs every five seconds or so. I did this for a minute, and then for another, but she failed to respond. Just as I was about to give it a third and final try, she coughed quietly and then more violently, and expelled a lungful of fluid. Her eyes opened wide with shock and then closed again as I rolled her over, and with a mixture of sadness and relief in her voice she quietly whispered Julianne's name.

MY THOUGHTS RETURNED to Harold, and I quickly decided that I had to make one final try to release him. But I was tired and weak from my injury: before I'd gotten back to the kitchen I was already finding it difficult to stay above water.

As I sank, my body instinctively stopped struggling to move forward, and it seemed that everything within and around me slowed down to half its normal speed. My breath became calm and at peace rather than quickened in panic. My arms and legs lost their fatigue as I stopped working against the water and allowed myself to flow along with it. I opened my eyes and saw the same types of objects I'd seen a few minutes before, not as obstacles now but rather as partners in a slow, strange aquatic dance that I'd succumbed to despite my original intentions. I remember thinking, for the first time in recent memory, that I was satisfied. I knew how Langley had died, I knew the Crane family story, I had done something worthy in saving Martha's life, I had become reconciled with Mindy: all these things gave me a feeling of deep peace that turned my attention to what was about to come.

I closed my eyes again and quickly forgot about Harold, indeed forgot about everything life-related that had once concerned me, until I was shocked out of my near-death journey by a hand reaching down through the water and grabbing the collar of my shirt. It was a hand I'd seen and felt before, a strong hand attached to a strong female body that I had once known well but wanted nothing to do with now. She wanted me, though, whether to pay back a debt she believed she owed me or because her mother had ordered her to save me or simply because it was not God's will to have me yet. Whatever the explanation, I was not pleased with Julianne Radisson at that moment of interrupted peace. I blinked furiously to clear my eyes and breathed in air to clear my head, but I could not express my displeasure, could say nothing at all, in fact, because a few seconds after my forced emergence I fell unconscious.

Chapter Sixteen

At last the secret is out,
as it always must come in the end.
The delicious story is ripe
to tell to the intimate friend.

—W. H. Auden, "At Last The Secret Is Out", 1936

FOR FIVE DAYS I LAID IN A HOSPITAL BED recovering from an acute case of hypothermia, alive, my doctor told me, only because Julianne Radisson, herself half-drowned and nearly frozen, had removed my wet clothes, wrapped me in dry blankets, and held me close until Stephen Delaney and an EMT team rescued us and her mother from the second floor of Crane's End and pulled Harold Radisson's corpse from the water.

I was semi-conscious at best for most of that five-day span. When I finally came to I remembered bits and pieces of visits and conversations that seemed to me a confusing mosaic of faces and an indecipherable cacophony of voices. Actual events and dreams blended together: I remember thinking that Louie had been shot, that Julianne had perished in the flood, that Harold Radisson himself had lowered Martha and me into a boat and rowed us to higher ground. My most distinct vision was of an Iroquois woman standing on the far shore of the Mohawk, a glowing phantom beckoning me forward through the darkness and rain, chiding me for not showing her enough gratitude for having saved me. I was full of questions, hysterical with fears, and my doctor, Dr. Shaughnessey, responded by administering dose after dose of a very effective sedative.

Dr. Shaughnessey also called Stephen Delaney, perhaps on the detective's insistence, and I woke up on Saturday morning with both men in the room, thinking that my hospital bed had been wheeled to the Hibernian Hall on Adams Street. I made a comment to that effect and both Delaney and Shaughnessey laughed.

"Humor is the best sign of recovery," Dr. Shaughnessey said as he walked towards the door. "Steve, buzz me if he goes haywire again."

Delaney sat and stared my way for a long time, a slight smile on his face and his hands perfectly still.

"What's going on in the world?" I finally said.

"Same old, same old," he said with irony.

"How's Louie?"

"Busy as ever cleaning up the Patriot Village mess."

I sat up, dizzy with a headache. "Cleaning up?"

"The site was flooded with six feet of water. When H. Paul Gass saw how bad the damage was, he pulled his money out. The other investors followed. Louie, of course, got the clean up job, along with a dozen others citywide."

"Patriot Village isn't being built?"

Delaney shook his head.

"What happened to Crane's End?" I asked.

"The Radisson house? It's beyond repair. What the flood didn't ruin was destroyed by an electrical fire two days later." Delaney paused. "Seems like Josephine Strong finally got her revenge."

I thought I was dreaming again. "What did you say?"

"Martha told me the whole story. If she weren't a professional historian, I'm not sure I'd believe it." He hesitated then said, "You haven't asked about Julianne yet. The evidence I gathered shows that she was perfectly justified in administering Langley's medication. She lied to us about her uncle and the vodka, of course, but that was under duress. The DA wouldn't dare file charges given everything that's happened, especially since she's something of a hero having saved you."

"I should talk with her."

Delaney shook his head. "We don't know where she is. She and Martha both left town after Harold's funeral. Martha told me they were going to travel and get to know each other, and then settle down in DC or Baltimore. But she didn't tell me where they were traveling to or for how long they'd be gone. They just took the insurance money and ran."

"Is Martha in trouble?"

"The embarrassment is trouble enough. There's no way Martha Radisson'll work in higher education again."

"Embarrassment? Did their story go public?"

"A reporter named Freddie Teed got the exclusive. He mentioned you quite a lot, gave you most of the credit for uncovering the tale. He came here the other day, in fact, hoping you'd be awake. He said he used to work for your father."

"Langley wrote a statement," I said.

"We found it in a safe deposit box. The second of Teed's three articles quotes extensively from it. Langley had a lot of anger bottled up inside him, Tom, mostly directed towards the Radissons. I can't say I'd envy him."

I remembered my conversation with Martha as we drove to Crane's End and realized that I still couldn't answer the question, first posed by Mindy, of how well I really knew the man.

"Did Langley know Crane's story?"

"That it was Crane's daughter who killed him? No, sadly, he didn't. He died thinking it was a Republican. But he knew he had a daughter in Julianne. He spelled it out in his statement along with everything else that happened in the early '70s."

"Did Teed print that?"

"Yes. But only with Martha's permission, and only after she told Julianne."

"So Julianne knows. How did she take it?"

"I don't know."

I had so many questions, there was so much to catch up on, that I didn't know what to say next. Delaney sensed this and said, "Jens Erlenmeyer is as busy as Louie. He's been gearing up the Crusaders for their next battle against dredging the river for PCBs. I arranged to have his visa extended another year in return for causing him so much trouble. And the university president stopped by just yesterday. He wants you to call him when you're up to a visit."

"You're a good secretary," I said.

"Not me. One of the nurses has been keeping track of everyone who's visited or called. There's more. Alexa says she enjoys teaching your class. Dr. Whittaker promises that you'll still get paid. Someone named Ray—he wouldn't leave his last name—gives you his best. Rasheed Wallace wants to buy you a drink. And Mindy McDonnell called three times and she's stopped by almost every day. She told the nurse to—"

"Call me the minute you regain consciousness."

Delaney and I both looked at the door and saw Mindy standing there wearing her long wool coat and a knit hat. Delaney smiled, then tossed the slips of pink paper back down on the table. "I've probably got my own pile of these to go through," he said. "See you soon, Tom."

With Delaney gone Mindy moved the chair away and sat on the edge of the bed. She looked at me for a moment and touched the bandage around my arm that held the I.V. in place. I watched a single tear roll down her cheek and catch on the edge of her smile.

"Did you see Freddy Teed's articles?"

"Yes. They're in the pile over there." She motioned towards a stack of books and newspapers on a table near the window. "I brought your Bible, too."

She handed it to me, and for a moment I was tempted to open and point. But I knew what words I needed for a change, and I turned to the fortieth Psalm. With Mindy still by my side I read aloud,

> *I waited patiently for the LORD,*
> > *He turned to me and heard my cry.*
> *He lifted me out of the slimy pit,*
> > *out of the mud and mire;*
> > *He set my feet on a rock*
> > *and gave me a firm place to stand.*
> *He put a new song in my mouth,*
> > *a hymn of praise to our God.*
> *Many will see and fear,*
> > *and put their trust in the LORD.*

MINDY WAS SILENT for a moment, then when I closed the Bible she said, "I talked with Julianne before she left town, Tom. She said to tell you she was sorry. She said she should have told you everything about Langley at the outset. I just thanked her for you and wished her good luck."

"Where did they go?"

"She didn't say."

"Did she seem OK?"

Mindy shrugged, then leaned forward and ran her hand through my hair. After a moment's hesitation she said, "We have a spare room, Tom. My mother and father both want you to stay there."

"Mindy . . ."

"You can study for your exam. Recuperate. There's nothing for you here anymore. Give me a list of books and I'll get them for you. You'll have plenty of peace and quiet. You can read in the Florida room . . ."

Growing tired, I reached up and placed a finger to her lips. "Mindy, do you want me there?"

"Yes."

My answer was the same, but I didn't respond because I suddenly fell asleep as Mindy gave hers. Fifteen minutes of consciousness, it seemed, was enough after five days of oblivion.

I REMEMBER DREAMING about Julianne that night. She was standing on the far bank of the Mohawk, naked in a cold fog, and when I looked closely I could see that she was an exact double of Josephine Strong—of Cornflower's ghost— who'd been in my previous dreams. I could also see Langley in her eyes, in her lips, mostly in her jet-black hair. She smiled and motioned for me to join her on the other side, and as I started to move forward her smile contorted itself into the ugly scowl of my old nemesis, the scarecrow. I was shocked and scared, but I was hypnotized too and wanted to see if it was really Julianne. Then a voice of warning from inside stopped me, and after a moment's hesitation I turned and walked away.

Later on I dreamed of my father. He was sitting in a lawn chair near the dock of our cottage on Wellesley Island, sipping a Bloody Mary and watching the boats criss-cross on the river. He was pontificating as he often did, telling me about the newspaper business, about how difficult it was to keep an independent mind in a world populated by ideologues, sycophants, and schemers. He said it was still the most rewarding business there was, though, and hoped that someday I'd follow his footsteps into it. Then he stood up, walked towards the dock, and motioned for me to join him.

"How's that professor you're so fond of?" he said when I got there.

"He died in a car accident. Congressman Radisson was involved."

"Harold Radisson always did have a streak of crooked-ness about him."

"I know," I said.

"Come on," my father said, and hopped into the Lyman.

I untethered the boat as he checked the gear and started the motor, and then I got in. He opened the throttle and we went around the northwest end of Wellesley Island and into Canadian territory, into the most beautiful section of the river I knew. The water was cold and clear with dozens of tightly packed islands that presented trouble to many inex-perienced boaters, but not to my father. He weaved around a few of the smaller ones, passed through a deep, narrow channel, and stopped the boat alongside one island that rose high and straight out of the water. He cut the engine and dropped anchor, and pulled two cans of Genesee beer out of a cooler and popped them open.

"Harold Radisson's dead," I said. "Drowned in his own home." I watched my father remove his shirt, exposing the strong arms, barrel chest and expanding belly that I re-membered from childhood. "I left him there, Dad. I left him there to die."

He drank his beer and crushed the empty can with his hand. "It's not for you to decide whether or not that was a mistake, Tom."

Then he smiled and called me a hero for saving Martha's life, which he said he'd read about in the paper, and re-minded me that I still wasn't half the man he was. To prove it he stood up tall and challenged me to race him to a buoy about a hundred yards away. And then, with a white swell moving across the blue-green water and lapping against the granite cliffs beside us, with seagulls above us playfully rid-ing the breeze, I lifted off my shirt and dove into the water, only a second behind my father, feeling, in my dream, cleansed and happy and whole.

About the Author

Thomas Pullyblank was born and raised in rural upstate New York. Having earned degrees in history at the University at Albany and a Master of Divinity degree from the Boston University School of Theology, Pullyblank now teaches history at the SUNY College at Oneonta and serves as a United Methodist pastor near Cooperstown, New York. He lives on a small working farm with his wife and son. This is his first novel. He is currently working on a second upstate New York historical mystery featuring Tom Flanagan.

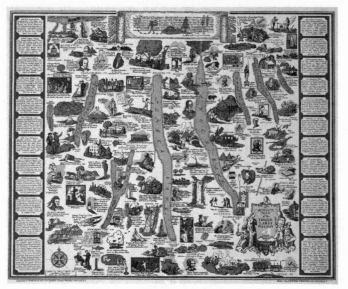